THE GUNSMITH

471

A Price on a Gunsmith's Head

THE GUNSMITH

471

A Price on a Gunsmith's Head

J. R. Roberts

SPEAKING VOLUMES, LLC
NAPLES, FLORIDA
2021

A Price on a Gunsmith's Head

ISBN 978-1-64540-514-6

Chapter One

Clint Adams heard the shot, felt the bullet whiz past his ear, and immediately threw himself from the saddle. He landed on his left hip with a bone-jarring thud and rolled off the road into a dry wash. His Tobiano ran off to a safe distance and then stopped to wait.

Clint drew his gun and looked around trying to locate the shooter. From the sound of the shot, it had come from a rifle, which meant it was probably fired from a distance. His pistol wouldn't do him any good, and his rifle was on his saddle. He holstered his gun and rubbed his sore hip.

He'd been shot at many times before. It usually meant somebody had recognized him and wanted to make a name for themselves, even if they had to shoot the Gunsmith in the back. After all, look how famous Jack McCall was for shooting Wild Bill Hickok in the back of the head.

Clint had some options. He could stand, hoping to draw fire again and locate the shooter. Or he could simply stay where he was and wait the shooter out. Whoever it was would become impatient and either come after him or leave.

It was midday and the Arizona sun was high. It was only going to get hotter. He decided to stay where he was and see what happened. Besides, his hip was killing him, and he didn't think he could move around very well, at the moment.

He looked over at the Tobiano, who was standing calmly. He only hoped the shooter wouldn't decide to change targets.

After two hours he thought he should move. If he waited any longer, he might not be able to move his left leg at all. He flexed it, then decided to try to put his weight on it. Gingerly, he stood, ready to duck if there was another shot. He put his weight on the leg, and it held. His next step was to walk to the Tobiano. If the shooter was still waiting, he would have a free shot while Clint was out in the open.

He started walking, looking around to see if he could spot the shooter. He reached the Tobiano safely, picked up his reins and turned him.

"You're a good boy, Toby," Clint said, stroking his neck. "Most horses would've run off at the sound of the shot."

He put his left foot in the stirrup and, even though it was painful, mounted up. There was still no shot.

"All right," Clint said, "let's go, Toby. I need to find out if my hip's broken."

A Price on a Gunsmith's Head

***

The next town Clint came to was called Surprise, about twenty-seven miles north of Phoenix. It was small but appeared busy as he rode down the main street. Folks paused to look at him but paid only a moment's attention before going back to their daily tasks.

A man was outside the mercantile sweeping the walk with brisk strokes. Clint rode up to him. The man stopped and looked up.

"Help you, friend?" he asked.

"Do you have a doctor in town?" Clint asked.

"We do," the man said. "Keep going for two more streets. He's got an office above the hardware store. You'll see his shingle."

"Much obliged," Clint said.

"You don't look injured," the man said.

"I fell off my horse," Clint said. "I just want to get checked out."

"Well, Doc Hawes is your man."

"Thanks, again."

Clint directed the Tobiano down the street until he saw the shingle hanging on the side of the hardware store. He reined in and dismounted painfully. His leg and hip had stiffened up during the ride.

He tied the Tobiano to a hitching post and went to the alley next to the hardware store. There was an outside stairway that led to the doctor's office. It was fifteen steps, and he took them one at a time, trying to keep as much weight as he could off his left leg and hip.

When he reached the top of the stairway, he knocked on the door. It was opened by an attractive woman in her thirties.

"Yes?"

"I'd like to see Doc Hawes, if he's here," he said. "Are you his nurse?"

She smiled.

"I'm not his nurse," she said, "I'm him. I mean, I'm Doc Hawes. Can I help you?"

"Oh, I'm sorry," he said, "I didn't know—I fell off my horse, Doc. I think I might've broken something."

"Well, come on in," she said, "and we'll take a look and see."

He limped into the office, which was small and very clean.

"Now what hurts?" she asked.

"My left leg and hip. I landed on them."

"Well then," she said, "you better get those pants off…"

Chapter Two

Clint got his trousers down around his ankles, but Doc Hawes wanted them off completely. He removed his boots, set his gunbelt aside, and took off his pants while seated on her examining table.

"Your underwear, too, please," she said.

"Is that really necessary?" he asked.

"Don't tell me you're shy."

He slid his underwear off, sat there naked from the waist down.

"Wow," she said, "that's quite a bruise." She touched his hip with her fingertips, causing him to catch his breath from the pain. The bruise was as wide as her hand.

"Now just relax," she said. She examined his leg, holding it, flexing it several times. "Your leg's not broken."

She was a pretty woman, she smelled good, and her touch was tender. He couldn't help himself, and his cock started to get hard. He knew she had to notice, but he never saw her look at him.

"All right," she said, "let's see about this hip."

She probed it with her fingers, causing him pain, and made him flex his leg again.

"It's very bruised," she said, "but I don't believe you broke anything. How did this happen?"

"I fell off my horse."

"Just clumsy?" she asked.

"No," he said, "somebody took a shot at me."

"That sounds like something you should talk to the sheriff about," she said.

"I intend to, but I thought I'd come and see you—a doctor—first."

"You can get dressed," she said. This time he thought he saw her steal a glance at his cock as he was pulling his underwear back on, then his pants.

"Your leg will be stiff for a few days," she said. "That hip's gonna be sore even longer. I can give you something for the pain—"

"That's okay," he said, tucking his shirt in. "I'm just glad nothing's broken."

"I would recommend you not ride for a few days," she said. "The hotel down the street usually has rooms available."

"I'll probably do that," he said, strapping on his gun. "What do I owe you, Doc?"

"A dollar."

He paid her.

"If you want to come and see me again before you leave town," she told him, "I won't charge you again."

For a moment Clint wondered if she was being professional or not.

"I'll keep that in mind," he said.

"Would you mind telling me my patient's name?" she asked.

"It's Clint Adams."

She looked surprised.

"Well, I guess that might be a reason why somebody took a shot at you."

"You're probably right," he said. "Thanks for the help, Doc."

"Remember," she said, "if you want something for the pain, come back and see me."

"I'll remember." He went to the door, stopped with his hand on the doorknob. "Can you direct me to the sheriff's office?"

"Of course," she said. "Go out, turn left and go one street. The office will be across the way."

"What's his name?"

"Sheriff Ned Fletcher," she said. "He's been the law here for a lot of years. He's sure to know who you are."

"Thanks, again, Doc."

"Anytime, Mr. Adams," she said. "Come back any time."

He left and went down the stairs, gingerly.

***

Since the doctor said the sheriff's office was only one more block, Clint decided to walk rather than climb back aboard Toby. He thought it might help work the stiffness out.

He drew some more looks from locals, maybe because of the Tobiano, maybe because he was limping, or perhaps simply because he was a stranger.

When he found the sheriff's office, he tied the horse to the post out front, mounted the boardwalk and knocked on the door.

"Come!" a man shouted.

Clint opened the door and entered.

"I can tell you're a stranger without even lookin' up," the lawman said. He was staring down at some wanted posters spread across his desk.

"How's that?" Clint asked.

Sheriff Ned Fletcher looked up at him. He was in his fifties, with a weathered, heavily lined face, deep-set, gray eyes and a heavy gray mustache that hid most of his mouth.

"You knocked," he explained. "Nobody in this town knocks on my door. What can I do for you, Mister?"

"Sheriff, my name's Clint Adams."

"Well," Fletcher said, sitting back, "this should be interestin'. Have a seat, Mr. Adams, and tell me what the Gunsmith is doin' in my town?"

Chapter Three

"Somebody took a shot at me just outside of town," Clint explained.

"That why you limped in here?" Fletcher asked.

"Yes," Clint said. "They missed, but I took a tumble from my horse, landed on my hip."

"You should probably see our Doc," Fletcher said.

"I just came from Doc Hawes," Clint said. "Nothing's broke, but she recommends I don't ride for a few days."

"That's a damn shame," Fletcher said.

"Why's that?"

"It means you're gonna have to walk out of town."

"I don't get you, Sheriff."

Fletcher sat forward again, clasped his hands together on the desk.

"I don't want you in my town, Adams," he said. "I'm tellin' you to leave."

"I can't leave," Clint said. "And I certainly can't walk."

"Well then, you're gonna have to try and ride. Go to Phoenix, where you'll be able to hide for a while. In a town like Surprise, you're gonna stick out. I don't know who took a shot at you outside of town, but somebody's sure to get the idea if you stay *in* town."

"You got somebody that stupid here, Sheriff?" Clint asked.

"Adams," the sheriff said, "there's somebody that stupid in every town."

"Well," Clint said, "you're asking a lot of me if you want me to leave town now."

"I tell you what," Fletcher said. "Spend the night and leave first thing in the mornin'."

That would give him time for a meal, a beer, some sleep, and breakfast before he would have to mount up again. He had no idea how he was going to feel come morning but decided not to argue the point now.

"That sounds like a plan, Sheriff," he said, getting to his feet.

"You think whoever took the shot recognized you in the last town you were in?"

"That's possible," Clint said, "but I've been on the trail for three days. Why wait that long to bushwhack me?"

"Well," Fletcher said, "they could have just recognized you on the trail."

"From a distance?" Clint said. "I don't think so."

Fletcher shrugged, "I hope you find out who it was before they make another try. And if they do, I hope it's not here in town."

"You and me both," Clint said. If the shooter tried again, he hoped it would be when he was healthy. With this bum leg and hip, he might have a hard time avoiding the bullet next time.

"Thanks, Sheriff."

He limped out of the lawman's office.

***

He went to the Palace Hotel, which Doc Hawes had mentioned. He got a room with no problem, then asked the clerk if there was somebody around who could take his horse to the livery.

"I'm a little gimpy at the moment, after an accident," Clint explained.

The middle-aged clerk said, "Of course, Sir. I have a boy who can take it over."

"Good," Clint said. "Thank you. When is your dining room open?"

"All day long, Sir," the clerk said. "We're at your disposal."

"Thanks, again."

There were no rooms on the first floor, so Clint had to painfully climb the stairs. When he got to the room, he found it small but clean with a comfortable bed. He sat on it but didn't have time to actually get comfortable. He was too hungry for that. He would've had the clerk have somebody take his saddlebags and rifle to his room so he could eat, but he wanted to wash up first. After all, he had been rolling around in a ditch. It might not have been a bad idea to change his shirt, as well.

Feeling cleaner and refreshed after using the pitcher-and-basin on the dresser top, he put on that fresh shirt and went back down to the lobby. As he entered the dining room, he saw it was about half full with what looked to be hotel guests. He had no trouble getting himself a table that was away from the door and windows.

"How are your steaks?" he asked the waiter.

"Depends on how you want it cooked," the waiter said.

"Bloody."

"I'll see what I can do. Potatoes and onions okay?"

"Perfect. And I'll have some coffee."

"Comin' up," the waiter said.

The small, fiftyish man went to the kitchen, came back with a cup and a pot of coffee, put them both on the table. Clint poured himself a cup and gratefully drank it. He was going to put off having a beer until after supper.

He felt himself relaxing as he waited for his steak, but he couldn't afford to completely relax while there was somebody nearby who wanted to kill him.

Chapter Four

The steak was bloody but that didn't mean it was good. Edible was about all Clint could call it. Surprisingly, though, the potatoes and onions were done to perfection.

"Well," the waiter asked, "what'dja think?"

"Must be someplace in town I can get a better steak," Clint said, "but the vegetables were great. I'm afraid to ask about your pie."

"Pie's good," the waiter said. "Our cook is more of a baker anyway."

"What do you have?"

"Apple and rhubarb, today."

"I hate rhubarb," Clint said. "I'll take the apple."

"Don't blame ya," the waiter said. "Not partial to rhubarb myself. I'll bring you your pie with some more coffee."

"Thanks."

The waiter turned out to be right. Whoever was in the kitchen was a better baker than a cook. The apple pie was perfect.

After supper Clint paid his bill then asked the waiter, "Where's the closest saloon?"

"Well, we ain't got one here in the hotel, more's the pity. The Cactus is the closest, but it ain't the best. For that you wanna go about three blocks to the Winchester."

"What's wrong with the Cactus?"

"No gamblin' and no music."

"They got beer?"

"Well, sure."

"That's good enough. Thanks."

***

Clint left the hotel and walked to the Cactus Saloon. It was small, clean, and quiet. Those were three things that did not attract people, so it was also pretty empty, which suited him. Clint limped to the bar.

"Help ya?" the friendly looking bartender asked.

"Beer."

The bartender drew the beer and set it in front of Clint. The Cactus also had clean glasses.

"You don't mind me sayin'," the barman commented, "you look a little worse for wear."

Clint sipped the cold beer and said, "Fell off my horse."

"Ouch, yeah, that'd do it."

Clint looked around.

"Always this quiet?"

"Pretty much," the man said. "We're too clean for the real drinkers and gamblers."

"A clean saloon suits me, especially when it includes the glasses."

"If you come in tonight, we'll have a girl workin' the floor," the bartender said, "but that's about it. No music, no gamblin' "

"That's what I was told."

"The clerk at the hotel?"

"Yeah."

"He probably told you to go to the Winchester."

"He did."

The bartender nodded.

"That place has got everythin' we don't," the man said, "includin' trouble."

"Well, luckily I'm just lookin' for a quiet beer," Clint said.

"Gonna be in town long?"

Clint didn't tell the man the sheriff told him to leave in the morning.

"The doc says I shouldn't ride until my hip heals," he said.

"The doc," the man said, his eyes brightening. "Seein' her is worth fallin' off a horse."

"Does she ever come in here?" Clint asked.

"Oh sure, she has a drink now and then," the bartender said.

"What about the sheriff?"

"He favors the Winchester, like most of the men in town."

That suited Clint, too. He didn't want to run into the sheriff, as it was very likely he wasn't going to leave town in the morning.

After one beer, Clint paid and said, "Thanks."

"Come on by later," the bartender said. "Ruby's pretty cute."

"I'll try to make it," Clint said and limped out the door.

***

As he walked through the hotel lobby, he exchanged a nod with the clerk. He had stayed alert during the walk from the saloon to the hotel. Even though some of the townspeople paid him some attention, nobody seemed intent on his progress. A quick check of rooftops and windows revealed no rifle barrels.

In his room he checked his window, saw that it overlooked the alley next to the hotel with no access from outside. He removed his gunbelt, hung it on the bedpost, and dropped onto the bed gratefully, taking the weight off his leg and hip.

The exertions of the day, and his injury, got to him, and he was asleep in minutes.

Chapter Five

When he woke the next morning, he tried to sit up in bed and immediately regretted the decision. He had forgotten about his hip and leg.

He settled back down, waited for the pain to subside, then tried again, but slowly. This time he got both feet down on the floor and sat like that for a few minutes before standing.

"Stupid," he said. He could have landed better and rolled avoiding injury. He had done it before. He was getting too old to be leaping from the saddle.

He washed his face, hands, and torso before dressing gingerly. Pulling his boots on was a struggle, but he managed. He strapped on his gun and left his room.

In the lobby he asked the clerk, "Where can I get a good breakfast?"

"Not here, that's for sure," the man said. "Try down the street, the Lotus Blossom Café. I think you'll like it."

"Thanks."

"Just go out and make a left."

Clint waved and limped out the door.

He found the Lotus Blossom with no trouble. It had a large flower drawn on the window. It looked like a rose to him, though.

Inside he found about half of the ten tables occupied.

"Sit anywhere you like," the waitress called to him. "I'll be with you in a minute."

The window tables were taken, because that's where normal people liked to sit. But people who liked their privacy, like the Gunsmith, liked the back tables.

While he was waiting for the waitress to serve, a woman entered the café, saw him and walked over.

"Are you stalking me?" Doc Hawes asked.

"I just thought I'd stop in for breakfast," Clint said. "The desk clerk at the hotel recommended the place."

"I was kidding," she said. "I have breakfast here every day."

"Will you join me, then?"

"Why not?" she said and sat across from him. "Have you taken my advice?"

"Which advice?"

"About not riding for a while."

"I thought I would," Clint said, "but the sheriff has ordered me out of town today."

"That's not right," she said. "You can't ride."

"He told me to walk."

"I'll talk to him," she said. "You keep your hotel room."

The waitress came over.

"Friend of yours, Doc?" she asked.

"This is Clint, Flora," Doc Hawes said. "We'll both have your special omelette." She looked at Clint. "You'll love this."

"Sounds great," Clint said. "Can I wash it down with coffee?"

"Of course," Doc Hawes said. She looked at Flora. "Two coffees, strong."

"Bring a pot," Clint said.

"Comin' up," the middle-aged waitress said.

"She'll bring some biscuits, too," Doc Hawes said. "She always does. And doesn't charge me."

"You save her life once?"

"Not quite," Doc said. "I treated her and she couldn't pay me. This is her way."

Flora brought the pot of coffee, two cups and, as Doc Hawes predicted, a basket of biscuits.

"Omelettes in a couple of minutes," she promised.

"So tell me," Clint said, "why's the sheriff going to let me stay in town on your say so?"

"Why do you think?" she asked, with a sly smile.

"He owes you, too?"

"Not exactly."

"Don't tell me the old goat is in love with you."

"Now you're close."

"What?"

She laughed.

"The old goat is my father," she said. "Hawes is my married name."

"So," Clint said, "maybe there's a chance I can take a few days to heal."

"I would say so, Mr. Adams," Doc Hawes said, "I would say so."

***

After breakfast Doc Hawes suggested that they go and see the sheriff together. When they entered the office, the sheriff looked up from his desk.

"Why doesn't this surprise me?" he asked.

"This man is my patient, and I've advised him to stay in town until he heals."

"How long is that gonna take?" the lawman asked.

"I don't want him riding for at least a few days," she said.

"Did he tell you what happened?" the sheriff asked. "Why he fell off his horse?"

"Yes, he did," Doc Hawes said, "and as our town sheriff I'd think you'd be looking into the matter."

"Do you know who he is?" Sheriff Fletcher asked.

"I do," she said, "but that doesn't matter. I'm only concerned about his injuries."

Fletcher sat back in his chair, looking defeated.

"Oh, all right," he said, then leaned forward and pointed a finger at Clint. "Don't kill anybody while you're here."

"I'll do my best, Sheriff," Clint promised.

Chapter Six

As Clint and Doc Hawes left the sheriff's office she asked, "How was that?"

"Very impressive," he said. "I get the feeling you're the law in town, not him."

"That's not true," she said, "but I can get him to do what I want when it's medically necessary."

"I guess I should go back to my hotel room, then," Clint said.

"Not necessarily," she said. "I think you should probably walk a while."

"Walk?"

"Yes," she said, "work that stiffness out."

"Well," he said, "if that's what the doctor orders."

"It is," she said. "In fact, I think I'll walk with you, for a while." She linked her arm through his left one.

"Then maybe you should lead the way," he said.

"We're not going anywhere special," she told him. "Just walk."

They started walking down the street.

"Tell me," she said, "when somebody takes a shot at you like they did yesterday, don't you get an urge to, maybe, change your life?"

"It's a little late for that," Clint said. "Even if I tried, people wouldn't let me."

"But that's no way to live."

"Sometimes," Clint said, "you just don't have a choice."

They continued to walk, and he found out that her husband, a drunk, had been responsible for his own shooting death, blowing off the top of his head while cleaning a shotgun.

"That's a damn shame," he said.

"Actually," she said, "he saved me from doing the same thing."

"Blowing your head off?"

"No," she said, "his."

***

They continued to walk until they were standing in front of her shingle.

"I have to go to work," she said. "I have patients."

"What do you want this patient to do, Doc?"

"Stay alive," she said. "That probably means stay off the street."

"I'll do my best, Doc," he promised.

"Come in and see me later his afternoon," she suggested, "and I'll look you over."

Once again he wasn't sure her suggestion wasn't an "invitation."

"I'll do that."

She went inside, and he headed for his hotel.

When the first shot came, he forgot about his sore hip and leg and dove for cover, just as the second shot sounded.

He found himself behind a horse trough, gun in hand, looking around to see where the shots had come from. The people outside had run for cover, so the street was now empty.

He searched rooftops and windows, and the doorways across the way. Whoever it was, they had taken their two shots and then vanished.

He heard someone approaching, looked down the street and saw Doc Hawes.

"Stay back!" he shouted.

She stopped, spotted him, then nodded and ran into a doorway.

Someone was running from the other direction, and he turned and saw Sheriff Fletcher. He stood to meet him.

"I promised not to kill anybody," he said, "but somebody has different ideas."

***

In the sheriff's office, Fletcher watched as his daughter, Doc Hawes, checked Clint over.

"See? This was what I was afraid of if you stayed in town," the lawman said.

"It's not his fault somebody's shooting at him, Pa," Doc Hawes said.

"It's not?" Fletcher asked. "Then whose fault is it?"

"You're fine," she said to Clint, then turned to look at her father with her hands on her hips. "It's the fault of some crazy person."

"You think this was the same one who shot at you outside of town?" Fletcher asked.

"I hope so," Clint said. "I'd hate to think there are two people trying to kill me, right now."

"Well," Fletcher said, "I suppose all we can do is wait for them to try again and hope that this time you spot them."

"That's it?" she demanded. "That's all you can do?"

"That's okay, Doc," Clint said. "I'm figuring it that way, too."

"Well then, you're both crazy," she said, and stormed out of the office.

"She's excitable," her father said. "I suggest you go back to your hotel and stay off the street. I don't want some innocent bystander gettin' hurt."

"We feel the same way, Sheriff," Clint said, and left.

Chapter Seven

Clint went back to his room, removed his gunbelt and boots and set them aside. He sat on the bed with his back to the bedpost and crossed his arms. He had a book in his saddlebag, but didn't feel like reading, at the moment. He was concerned with who was taking shots at him. It certainly wasn't something new, but worrisome nevertheless.

The sheriff was right about one thing. The only way Clint was going to catch the shooter was to catch him in the act. But he couldn't let the shooter pick the time. There had to be some way he could control when it happened next. *If* it happened again. After two tries, the shooter might give up. On the one hand, that would be a good thing. But on the other hand, he would never find out who it was. And that was something he really wanted to know.

But he wasn't going to find out by staying in his room.

***

When the door to the sheriff's office opened again, Doc Hawes walked in alone.

"What brings you back here?" he asked.

"I wanted to talk to you about Clint Adams."

"What about him?"

"Are you trying to get him killed?" she asked.

"Why would I do that, Laura?"

"I don't know, Father," she said. "That's what I'm trying to find out."

"Look, I've agreed to let him stay til he heals. What more do you want?"

"I want you to find out who's trying to kill him," she said.

"How am I supposed to do that?" he asked. "Be reasonable. I'm a sheriff, not a detective. Besides, why are you so interested?"

"I'm interested in all my patients," she said. "You know that."

"Is that the only reason?" he asked. "Just because he's your patient?"

"Father," she said, frowning at him, "what other reason could there be?"

Before he could answer, she turned and huffed out of the office.

Fletcher sat back in his chair and shook his head. He had been hoping for a long time that his daughter would find herself a husband. He only hoped Clint Adams wouldn't be the one she chose.

All the more reason to get him out of town as soon as possible.

***

Clint decided he had to be on the street. It was the only way he was going to draw the shooter out. He pulled his boots back on painfully, strapped on his gun and left the room.

He stepped out of the lobby and stood in front of the hotel. His options were to walk around with a target on his back, or just sit in a chair right there on the porch and wait. Of course, he could also go to a saloon and let himself be seen.

"What are you doing?"

He turned and saw Doc Hawes approaching. When she reached him, she put her fists on her hips.

"You're supposed to be in your room," she said.

"Hiding?" he asked. "That's not my style."

"Resting," she said. "That was your doctor's order."

"I'm sorry, Doc," he said, "but the only way I'm going to find out who's shooting at me is to get him to do it again. Your father was right about that."

"My father's not right about anything," she said. "That's why my Ma left him years ago."

"I'm sorry to hear that," Clint said, "but at least he's got you."

"He doesn't listen to me," she said. "In spite of the fact he agreed to let you stay in town."

"He's probably hoping I'll get killed," Clint said.

"Why do you say that?"

"Because he's a lawman," Clint said, "and I'm a man with a reputation."

"Is that what you think of all lawmen?" she asked.

"Pretty much," he said. "The ones that aren't my friends."

"You have friends who are lawmen?"

"Are," Clint said, "used to be, yeah, I have a few."

"You're a strange man," she said, sitting in the chair next to him.

"Don't sit there."

"Why not?"

"If somebody takes another shot at me, they might hit you," he said.

"You're my patient," she said. "I've got to take care of you."

"I'm fine," he said. "You've done your job. Now you have to stay away from me."

"You didn't think that when we were eating together," she pointed out.

"That's because I didn't know the shooter was in town," he explained. "Now I do, and I can't risk you getting hurt."

"So then stay inside."

"Look, Doc," Clint said, "I can't ignore the fact that somebody has tried to kill me twice. It's going to happen again, and I've got to try and get control of the situation."

"By making a target out of yourself?"

"Pretty much, yeah."

"Sounds like men being stupid, if you ask me."

That surprised him.

"You mean me being stupid?"

"I mean you," she said, "the man shooting at you, and my father. I mean all men. They're just . . . stupid."

"I'm sorry you feel that way," he said, "but it would be kind of stupid for you to insist on being around me."

"You know what?" she asked. "You're absolutely right about that." She stood up. "Absolutely."

She stepped down off the hotel porch and walked angrily away. He was sorry about how the conversation had gone, but at least she wasn't near him, anymore.

Chapter Eight

Clint remained in front of the hotel for a couple more hours, then decided it was time to get lunch. Instead of looking for someplace to eat, he decided to just go back to the Lotus Blossom, where he had breakfast with Doc Hawes. If the shooter had spotted him there that morning, maybe he would see him again.

The waitress recognized him when he walked in.

"Same table again, Mister?" she asked.

"Sounds good."

She led him to the table.

"Are ya meetin' Doc Hawes again?" she asked.

"Not this time," Clint said. "I'll be having lunch alone."

"What'll it be, then?"

"Something hot," he said. "What do you recommend?"

"We do a really good beef stew."

"Then that's what I'll have."

"And to drink?"

"A cold beer."

"Comin' up."

He sat back and put his hat on one of the chairs at his table. Around him several of the other tables were occupied by townspeople. He didn't see anyone there who might fit the description of a shooter. But that didn't mean he wasn't outside.

So he decided he would eat a nice, leisurely lunch and then step outside and see what was waiting for him.

***

Sheriff Ned Fletcher entered the hotel and went to the front desk.

"Clint Adams," he said. "Is he in his room?"

"No, Sir."

"Do you know where he went?"

"All I know is he was sittin' out front all mornin'," the clerk said. "He left a little while ago."

"Okay," Fletcher said, "thanks."

He left the lobby and stopped just outside. It was too early for the saloon, so that meant Adams was either walking the streets, making a target of himself, or he went to lunch.

Fletcher tried two places before he saw Clint sitting at a table in the Lotus Blossom. He decided to go into the hardware store across the street and watch from the window. Maybe he would be able to spot somebody watching Adams.

***

"How was it?" the waitress asked.

"It was very good," Clint said. "Even better than you said it would be."

"So tell me," the woman said, "why aren't you havin' lunch with the Doc?"

"I think she might be mad at me," Clint said.

"That ain't the way I saw it."

"What do you mean?"

"I mean a woman don't look at a man the way she was lookin' at you, if she's mad at him."

"You've got it wrong," he said. "She treated me as a doctor. That was it. There's nothing else going on."

"You're a foolish man if you believe that, Mister," the waitress said.

He paid his bill and thought about what the waitress had said. He had to admit to himself, he thought the doctor might be interested in him, but he also thought that might have been his ego. Now, however, somebody else was pointing it out.

As Clint stepped out the front door of the Lotus Blossom, he saw a flash of light across the street.

Chapter Nine

Earlier that morning, Sam Tolliver and Dave Barron entered the Cactus Saloon. It was early enough for the place to be empty.

"Two beers," Tolliver said.

"You sure?" the bartender asked. "It's pretty early."

"He said two beers," Barron repeated.

The bartender studied the two men. While they were young, they were certainly old enough to drink.

"Suit yerself," he said, and gave them the beers.

They picked up the mugs and carried them to a table.

"How could you have missed?" Tolliver asked. "He was right there in the street."

"Hey!" Barron said. "You missed 'im out on the trail."

He drank some of his beer, sullenly.

"I think we got to do this proper," Tolliver said.

"Whataya mean?"

"I mean stop trying to bushwhack him, and just take him head on."

"He's the goddamned Gunsmith, Sam," Barron said. "You wanna get killed?"

"No," Tolliver said, "but I wanna collect this bounty that's on his head. And I know he's the Gunsmith, but he's gettin' old, Dave. Now, I'm pretty fast with a gun, and you're faster."

"I say let's try it one more time," Barron suggested. "He's sittin' in front of the hotel, bold as brass."

"I know," Tolliver said, "he's waitin' for us."

"Huh?"

"He's sittin' there hopin' we'll try again," Tolliver said.

"You really think that?" Barron asked.

"Yeah, I do."

"Then maybe we need help," Barron said.

"And split the bounty?" Tolliver asked. "I don't think so."

"So this idea of yours," Barron said, "takin' him head on. When and where?"

"Today," Tolliver said. "Let's get it over with."

"Just walk up to him at the hotel and say 'Hey, Mr. Gunsmith, we tried to kill you twice, and now we wanna do it right?' "

"Not exactly."

"Then what?"

"He's gotta eat, don't he?" Tolliver said. "Let's start by seeing if he goes back to that same café. All we gotta do is wait for him outside."

Barron thought about it, then finished his beer and said, "Okay, let's do it."

***

The flash was the sun glinting off the metal of a gun. Clint almost drew and fired but he held back. They hadn't fired, yet. Instead, two men stepped out from the doorways they were occupying and into the street.

"Adams!" one called.

"You the two cowards who tried to bushwhack me twice?" Clint asked.

"That's right," one said, "only now we decided to do it proper."

They were pretty young, and Clint knew it was going to be hard to talk them out of it.

"What's this about?" he asked.

"What's it have to be about?" the spokesman said. "You're the Gunsmith."

"That's the only reason?" Clint asked. "You want to die because of who I am?"

"Tell 'im, Sam," the other man said, "tell 'im about the money."

"Shut up, Dave!"

"What money?" Clint asked. "Is somebody paying you to kill me? Is that it?"

"Never mind," the man named Sam said. "That ain't important."

"It's important to me," Clint said. "If somebody's paying you, I want to know who it is."

"I told you, it ain't important!" Sam said. "Dave, just do it."

Clint looked at Dave and decided he was going to draw first. He was right. The young man went for his gun, and he was pretty fast.

Clint drew and fired, striking Dave Barron in the center of the chest. The shot drove him back a few feet with a shocked look on his face, and then onto his back in the street.

"Damn it—" Sam Tolliver said, grabbing for his gun.

"Don't!" Clint shouted, but it was too late. He didn't have a choice.

He shot Sam Tolliver, knocking the man right over onto his back with a chest shot.

Clint saw another man step into the street and recognized the sheriff. The lawman must have been watching the action from the hardware store he had just come out of. It could have been a coincidence that he was in there, but Clint doubted it.

Clint stepped into the street, ejected the two spent shells from his gun, reloaded and holstered it.

Chapter Ten

The Sheriff and Clint met over the bodies of the two men in the street.

"This is what I was afraid would happen," the lawman said.

"So you just stood by and watched," Clint said.

"What did you expect me to do?"

The sheriff crouched down and went through the dead men's pockets. He came out with a folded piece of paper.

"What's that?" Clint asked.

"Have a look," Fletcher said.

He handed it to Clint, who unfolded it. He was shocked by what he saw.

"Well?" Fletcher asked.

"It looks like a wanted poster," Clint said, "but it's not official."

"Let me see."

Fletcher took it and read: "One thousand dollars for the death of the Gunsmith."

He looked at the back, which was blank, and then the front again.

"This is crazy," Clint said.

"Let's get these bodies off the street and talk in my office," Fletcher said.

***

They headed for the lawman's office after the bodies had been taken to the undertaker. Doc Hawes tried to go with them, but her father stopped her.

"Just Mister Adams," he said.

"Pa—"

"That's final!"

She looked startled.

"Come on," Fletcher said to Clint.

They continued on.

In the sheriff's office the lawman opened a bottom drawer, took out a bottle of whiskey and two glasses. Without asking, he handed Clint one who did not decline.

"Have a seat," Fletcher said, and they each sat.

"How do we find out who printed that poster?" Clint asked.

"Let me see it," Fletcher said, and Clint handed it over. The lawman sat back in his chair and studied it.

"Usually it says who to contact," he said. "That's not on here."

"I noticed that."

"But sometimes you gotta read all the print . . ." Fletcher said, squinting.

"What do you mean?"

Fletcher handed the poster back. Clint squinted at the small print near the bottom.

"Does that say 'Bank of Windham?' "

"That's what I see," Fletcher said.

"Where the hell is the Bank of Windham?" Clint asked.

"I know there's a Windham, South Dakota," Fletcher said, "and there's a Windham Kansas."

"Well," Clint said, "I'd prefer to go to Kansas, but . . ."

"Who wants you dead in South Dakota, or Kansas?" the sheriff asked.

Clint thought a moment. He had spent more time in Kansas than up in South Dakota. Who in Kansas might want him dead? He had been with a few women there, but would a woman put a price on his head? He'd had run-ins with men there and they hadn't ended well. Some of those men didn't survive.

Okay, a thousand-dollar reward. Who from his past would have that much money? And who the hell hated him that much? The family of a man he killed? A woman he left behind?

"What are you gonna do, Adams?" Sheriff Fletcher asked.

"Well, I'm going to start in these two places," he said. "Windham, Kansas and Windham, South Dakota."

"Meanin' you're gonna leave town?"

"I sure am," Clint said. "Tomorrow."

"You be sure you tell my daughter that wasn't my idea," Fletcher said.

"Don't worry," Clint said. "I'll let her know." He put the empty glass down on the desk and stood up. "Thanks for the drink."

"Don't mention it."

As Clint went out the door, Fletcher was putting the bottle back in his desk.

***

When the knock came at his door, he had a good idea who it was going to be.

"Hello, Doc."

"May I come in?" she asked.

"Sure."

As she entered, she saw his saddlebags sprawled out on the bed.

"Getting ready to go somewhere?"

"I'll be leaving tomorrow," he said.

"Against your doctor's orders?" she demanded.

"Look at this," he said and handed her the poster.

"You're wanted?" she asked.

"It's not official," he said, taking it back. "Some private person put this out on me."

"Who would do something like that?"

"Somebody who hates me."

"And do you have any idea who that could be?"

"Yes and no," he said. "A lot of people have reasons to hate me. I just have to find the right one."

"One who can afford a thousand dollars," she said.

"That's right."

"And you feel you have to leave tomorrow."

"The quicker I get to the bottom of this, the quicker I can stop worrying who's the next shooter," he explained.

"I suppose I can understand that."

"Good," he said. "Your father wanted me to make sure you knew I wasn't leaving because of him."

She didn't reply to that, but simply turned and went to the door to make sure it was locked.

"You think locking me in is going to make a difference?" he asked.

"I think locking *us* in will," she said, and started to unbutton her shirt.

Chapter Eleven

"Doc—" Clint started.

"Laura," she said. "My name is Laura."

"Laura, look—"

"Oh, come on, Clint," she said, peeling the shirt off, "you knew where this was headed."

"Well," he said, "I suspected—"

"And you were right," she said, tossing her shirt aside. Beneath it she was naked. In her thirties, she had heavy breasts with dark nipples.

She moved closer to him and started to unbutton his shirt.

"Now, I know your hip and leg hurt, so you just have to lie back and let me do all the work," she said. Then she giggled and added, "Doctor's orders."

Since his gun and boots were already off, she only had to undo his trousers, then sit him on the edge of the bed so she could slide them off. Once she had tossed them across the room, she grabbed for his underwear and yanked them down.

"I'll bet you knew how unprofessional I was being, staring at this in my office," she said, touching his cock.

"It did occur to me."

"Well, now you know," she said, "I'm more interested in you than a doctor is a patient. But since you're leaving tomorrow, we need to get this over with tonight."

She grabbed his cock and began to stroke it, while he reached out and fondled her luscious breasts.

"You're still a little overdressed," he pointed out.

She stood up and he watched as she finished removing her clothes. When she came and joined him on the bed, he found his arms filled with opulent, smooth curves.

She kissed him while lying atop him, which trapped his evergrowing penis between them. Abruptly, he took hold of her and flipped her onto her back. From that position, he began to explore her body with his hands and mouth. He soon had her moaning and writhing in the throes of pleasure beneath him.

"Oh, God, what are you waiting for?" she asked.

He was waiting for her vagina to be good and wet, and when it was, he drove into her cleanly and easily. She took his hard cock to the hilt and the heat of her made him begin to sweat. He drove in and out of her, then, sliding his hands beneath her to cup her buttocks.

She wrapped her thighs around him, groped him with her hands, scratching his back with her nails.

He pumped in and out of her until they were each gasping for breath, and then finally exploded with a loud, guttural roar . . .

***

"Now this is something your father can never find out about," Clint said. "I don't need him coming at me with a shotgun."

"Oh, you've got the wrong father," she said. "He wouldn't care." She slid her hand over his belly as they lay side-by-side. "But still, it's not any of his business."

"That's good to hear."

She propped herself up on one elbow and looked down at him.

"Tell me, were you ever going to make a move if I didn't?" she asked.

"I'm sure I would have," he said, "after I healed."

"I'm sorry." She put her hand on his bruised hip. "Are you still in pain?"

"Some."

"Well," she said, sliding one thigh over him, "you should just lie there the rest of the night and let me take over."

"The rest of the night?" he asked, but he stopped talking when she took him into her mouth.

Chapter Twelve

The next morning Clint dressed slowly while Laura Hawes watched from the bed.

"I told you, you need to rest," she reminded him.

"That's not what you were saying most of the night," he pointed out.

"I was a woman while we were in bed," she said. "Now it's morning, and I'm a doctor, again."

He looked down at her nude body.

"You don't look like any doctor I ever knew," he said.

Abruptly, she pulled the sheet up to cover her nakedness.

"Is that better?"

He looked at the way the sheet molded itself to her.

"Not quite."

"Never mind," she said. "If you're going to ride today, you can't blame me for how you'll feel later tonight."

"I'm going to catch the train to Kansas City," he said. "I can rest there."

"So you've decided on Kansas first?" she asked. "Why?"

"I've been there more times than I've been to South Dakota," he said. "Chances are I offended someone."

"And if not Kansas, then you have to go all the way to South Dakota?"

"That would be my next step, yes."

"And after that?"

"I'll have to keep searching my memory for someone who might want me dead."

"This could take you a long time," she said.

"It could," Clint said, "but I can't just kill two men and forget it. I have to find out why."

"That's not the reputation I've heard about," she pointed out.

"Reputations very rarely stand up to be what they're supposed to be," Clint said. "Sorry if I disappointed you."

"Oh," she said, "I can't say that anything about our meeting has been disappointing."

"That's good."

He went to the bed and kissed her.

"Will you ever be coming back this way?" she asked.

"I don't know, Laura," he said. "I can't make any promises."

"I understand," she said, with a sigh.

He headed for the door, then stopped and turned back.

"If I don't come back, you won't ever send somebody out to kill me, will you?" he asked.

***

Clint walked slowly from the hotel to the livery. He was alert just in case there was still somebody around gunning for him. When he got there, he found Sheriff Fletcher standing at the front doors.

" 'mornin', Adams," the man said.

He wondered if the sheriff knew that he had spent the night with his daughter?

"Good-morning, Sheriff," Clint said. "Did you decide to see me off?"

"I suppose so," Fletcher said. "Just wanted to see that you got off okay. You know, without anybody else shootin' at you."

"I'm sure it's going to keep happening until I can get that thousand dollars withdrawn."

Clint studied the sheriff, wondering if the man was thinking about the thousand dollars, as well? Could he be tempted to try something while Clint was saddling his horse?

"Well," Clint said, "I better get going."

"I kind of thought Laura would be here to say good-bye to you," Fletcher said.

"I said goodbye to Doc Hawes last night," Clint said, "when she checked me over one last time."

"I see," Fletcher said, following Clint into the livery. "She give you a clean bill of health?"

"As a matter of fact, she didn't," Clint said. "She still says I shouldn't be riding, yet."

"I suppose you told her you didn't have a choice."

"That's exactly what I told her."

Clint got busy saddling the Tobiano, while the lawman continued to watch.

"I'm not going to hear the end of this," Fletcher said.

Clint stopped what he was doing and looked at Sheriff Fletcher.

"She seems like a fine girl," he said. "What does she have against you?"

"Ah, she blames me for her mother leaving the two of us," Fletcher said.

"That's a shame," Clint said.

He walked Toby out of the livery stable. The sheriff came up behind him.

"Well, I better get to my mornin' rounds," Fletcher said. "Good luck findin' whoever put that price on your head, Mr. Adams."

"Oh, I'll find them," Clint said. "You can believe in that."

Chapter Thirteen

By the time Clint got off the train in Kansas City, he had thought of two or three people who might hate him. Of course the question now was whether or not they still lived there.

Before looking for who he was thinking about, he collected Toby from the stock car. Then he went to a hotel near the station, the White Horse, where he had never stayed before. He was hoping to go as long as he could without being recognized. Down the street was a livery stable.

The next morning he would saddle up and head for Windham, Kansas.

But while he was in Kansas City there were two men and a woman he thought he would look for and talk to. But as he suspected, none of those three people were still in Kansas City. Now what he had to do was find out if any of them had moved to Windham.

He had supper in a small café he found several blocks from the White Horse Hotel, then went to his room, read for a while, and turned in.

***

The next morning he checked out, fetched his Tobiano from the livery, had breakfast in the same café,
then rode out of Kansas City. He figured Windham was
going to be about half a day's ride.

Unless someone at the train station or hotel had recognized him, he did not expect to be shot at while on the
trail, this time.

He didn't push Toby, since he figured to make
Windham that day, anyway. In fact, he stopped several
times to give the horse a blow. Once he sat on a rock
while the Tobiano drank from a water hole and thought
about all the gun battles he'd had over the years. How
many family members had been left behind? It could
even be that someone's child had matured and decided to
try to take vengeance. The number of people who might
hate him were countless. But of these, who could afford
to put a thousand-dollar price on his head were certainly
limited.

If he knew where his friends Bat Masterson and Luke
Short were these days, he would have sent them tele-
grams asking if they had heard anything. But the two
men seemed to be keeping a low profile of late, and he
had no idea where to find them.

What he liked about the Tobiano was the animal
knew when he'd had enough to drink. Clint didn't have
to stop him from drinking too much. When he finished,

Clint topped off his canteen, had a short drink, and then mounted up.

***

They made Windham close to dusk, and Clint noticed, as they rode down Main Street, that the Bank of Windham was closed. He would have to wait til the next morning when they opened.

Once again, as he had done many times before, he found a livery stable for the Tobiano, then walked back through town with his saddlebags and rifle, looking for a hotel. Windham was not a large town, but it seemed to be growing. He had passed two hotels along the way, chose one called The Windham West. He wondered if that meant that there was a Windham East somewhere in town.

He signed in at the front desk and accepted his key, without the clerk reacting to his name, which suited him. Hopefully, the man hadn't recognized him.

The first thing he wanted to do, since the bank was closed, was go and see the local sheriff, leaving his saddlebags and rifle in his room and went to the office he had seen while riding in.

As he entered, he saw a tall man bending over to touch his toes. He looked up as the door opened and then straightened. The badge on his chest gleamed, as if he had just polished it. His stiff back probably stemmed from the fact that he was in his fifties.

"I've got a stiff back," he said. "My doctor says I gotta stretch it."

"That should do it," Clint agreed.

"Can I help ya?" the lawman asked. "Oh, sorry. My name's Sheriff Jack Redmann."

"Clint Adams."

The two men shook hands.

"Have a seat, Mr. Adams," the lawman said. "Tell me what brings the Gunsmith to Windham."

"Have you ever seen this before?" Clint asked, passing the man the poster.

Redmann took it, examined it, then shook his head.

"Ain't never seen it before," he said, passing it back. "Doesn't look official, though. Some private citizen decide to put a price on your head?"

"I guess so," Clint said. "I'm trying to find out who it was."

"Why come here?" Redmann asked.

"It indicates on the bottom, in small print, that the money is in the bank of Windham."

"Here?" Redmann looked shocked.

"Well, either here or Windham, South Dakota. I'm checking here, first."

"I've been sheriff here for ten years," Redmann said. "Did you manage to come here before that and get someone hatin' you that much?"

"I've never been here, at all," Clint said. "I did know a few people in Kansas City, though." He reeled off three names. "Any of those folks live here?"

"Not to my knowledge," Redmann said, "and I pretty much know everybody in town."

"Well," Clint said, "I guess that just leaves me with checking the bank tomorrow."

"I better go with you," Redmann said. "That way you won't make anybody nervous."

"That suits me."

"Where are you stayin'?" Redmann asked.

"The Windham West."

"They have a good dining room," Redmann said. "Why don't I join you there in the mornin' for breakfast, and then we can walk over to the bank together. How about eight o'clock?"

"That suits me, too," Clint said, standing up. "I'll see you then."

He headed for the door, then turned and said, "Don't let that back stiffen up."

"I won't."

Clint left.

Chapter Fourteen

The next morning Clint was already seated at a table in the dining room when Sheriff Redmann entered.

"Sorry I'm late," the man said.

"No problem," Clint said. "I only ordered coffee."

When the waiter came over he said, " 'mornin', Sheriff. I didn't know this feller was a friend of yours."

"Hey, Leo," Redmann said. "Why don't you bring us two of Dorothy's specials."

"Comin' up."

As the waiter walked away Redmann said, "Dorothy's the cook, and she does a great steak-and-eggs."

"My favorite breakfast," Clint said.

Leo came back and poured coffee for both men, left a basket of biscuits on the table.

"I meant to ask you about that limp," Redmann said. "That got anythin' to do with somebody tryin' to kill you?"

"First time was while I was on my horse. When I jumped for cover, I landed on my hip. It's pretty bruised, and my leg is sore, but nothing's broken."

"Well, that's good."

When the steak-and-eggs came, Clint discovered why they called it their special. After they had both finished, Clint paid the bill and they walked to the bank.

The Bank of Windham was small. Inside were two desks and two teller's cages. In the back Clint could see the safe, standing with the door half open.

A woman seated at one of the desks brightened when she saw the sheriff.

"Can I help you, Sheriff?" she asked. She was middle-aged, pretty with a sunny smile. Her eyes shone as she gazed at the lawman.

"Yes, Miss Long," he said, "this gentleman would like to see the bank manager."

"Of course," she said. "I'll tell Mr. Clarendon that you're here."

She went into the bank manager's office, came back with that same, sunny smile.

"He'll see you now, gentlemen."

The sheriff led the way into the office, where a small, dapper man stood behind his desk.

"Sheriff," he said, "nice to see you."

"Mr. Clarendon, this is Clint Adams," the lawman said. "He has somethin' he wants to show you."

"How can I help you, Mr. Adams?"

Clint handed the man the poster, gave him a few seconds to peruse it.

"I don't understand," the manager said then.

"This is not an official wanted poster, Mr. Clarendon," the sheriff said. "Rather it's one that was put out by a private person."

"That's terrible," Clarendon said. "This could get somebody killed."

"It's already been tried," Clint said, "twice."

"Horrible!" the man said. "But why come to me?"

"At the bottom of the poster it indicates that the money will come from the Bank of Windham."

"What?" Clarendon adjusted his glasses on his nose and studied the poster again. "So it does. But . . . I can assure, you Mr. Adams, we have no involvement in this."

"That's what I wanted to know, Sir," Clint said, taking the poster back. "You see, there's a Windham, South Dakota, and they also have a bank with the same name."

"I didn't know that," the manager said.

"I was hoping to be saved a trip to South Dakota, but now it looks like I have no choice."

"I'm sorry we couldn't help you, Sir."

"That's all right," Clint said. "Thank you for seeing me. Good day."

"Good-day, Sir, Sheriff."

Clint turned and followed the sheriff out.

Chapter Fifteen

Outside the bank Redmann asked, "What's your next step gonna be?"

"A beer, a meal, and a night's sleep. Tomorrow I'll start for South Dakota."

"I'm sorry your trip here was for nothin," the lawman said. "I wish I could help."

"You can," Clint said. "Just keep your ears and eyes open. I'll let you know where I am, and you can send me a telegram if you hear anything."

"I'll do that," Redmann promised. "For that meal, I'd try Rochester's Steakhouse. The food's real good."

"Thanks, Sheriff."

"Sure thing," Redmann said. "If I hear anythin' while you're still here, I'll let you know."

"Much obliged."

The two men parted company, and Clint headed for the closest saloon to get that beer.

***

The saloon was called The Red Cactus, for some reason. It had a crude drawing of a red cactus above the door, and another over the bar. It was doing a brisk business for midday, but Clint was easily able to find room at the bar.

"Beer," he told the bartender.

"Comin' up," the friendly looking barkeep said.

As he set the beer down Clint asked, "What's the story with the red cactus?"

"The owner says he saw them in Brazil," the bartender said. "Me, I ain't never seen one."

"I believe I have," Clint said, "I just can't remember where."

"Ever been to Brazil?"

"As a matter of fact, I have."

"Maybe it was there."

The bartender moved down to serve another customer.

Clint drank his beer and stared at the crude drawing over the bar.

"Like it?"

He turned and looked at the woman who had sidled up next to him. She was brunette, attractive, in her thirties. She wore a red dress that was rather sedate for a saloon, not much skin showing. There were no other girls working the floor.

"It's kind of crude," Clint said, "but I actually do like it."

"I did it," she said.

"You drew that?"

She nodded.

"And the one outside?"

"Not bad," he said. "So you're the owner who saw the red cactus in Brazil?"

"That's me," she said. "Sadie Brandt." They shook hands. "What brings you to Windham?"

"I'm looking for someone."

"Oh? Who?"

"I don't really know," he said. "It's kind of a long story."

She looked around and said, "There's nobody else in here I want to talk to. Want to sit down?"

"Sure," Clint said. "Can I buy you a drink?"

"No," she said. "I own the joint, remember?" The bartender put a glass of champagne on the bar for her. She picked it up and said, "I have a table back here."

"Lead the way."

He followed her to the back of the room and through a curtained doorway. There was a table with four chairs in a small room. On the wall was another red cactus.

"These are all over the place," he observed.

"And in my dreams," she said.

"After seeing them in Brazil?"

She nodded.

"What took you to Brazil?"

"Money," she said.

"You got paid to go?"

"No," she said. "I was in a poker game, won a lot of money, and decided to travel. I went to Brazil, saw the red cactus there. Then I came back and bought this place."

"How long ago was that?"

"Five years."

"Still playing poker?" he asked.

"No," she said. "That was my last game."

"Why?"

She shrugged.

"How many times do you cash out that big?" she asked. "I decided to go out on a win." She raised her champagne glass and then drank. "What's your story?"

"Somebody tried to kill me recently," he said. "Twice."

"Is there a reason for that?"

"Normally I'd just say somebody recognized me and decided to make a name for themselves."

"And why would killing you make a name for some-body?" she asked.

"I'm Clint Adams."

"Ah," she said. "Tell me more."

Chapter Sixteen

"Somebody's put a price on my head," Clint said. "A thousand dollars to anybody who can kill me."

"Oh my God," she said. "Maybe I should've had Lenny, my bartender, poison you."

He stared at her.

"I'm kidding," she said. "So what brought you here to look for the person who put the price on your head?"

He took out the poster and handed it to her.

"Look at the bottom."

"The Bank of Windham," she said. "What did they say at the bank?"

"They don't know anything about it."

"Did you believe them?" she asked, handing it back.

"I don't have any reason not to," he said.

"So what are you going to do now?"

"There's another Bank of Windham," he said. "It's in South Dakota."

"That's a long way to go," she observed.

"I can't just walk around with this price on my head," he said. "I have to find out who put it there and get it removed."

"I can't say I blame you for that," she said. "So are you leaving in the morning?"

"Unless the sheriff turns up with something."

"He's a good man," she said. "Maybe he will."

He finished his beer.

"I'll pay for this on the way out," he said.

"Don't bother," she said. "It's on me. You tell an interesting story."

"So do you."

They both stood up.

"Look, you're going to want supper later," she said. "I know a good place, if you want some company."

"That sounds good," he said.

"Is eight too late?"

"Eight is fine," he said.

"Meet me back here, then," she said.

"I look forward to it."

They both left the back room, and as Clint walked past the bar, Sadie signaled the bartender that there would be no charge.

***

Under normal circumstances, Clint would have been happy to have met Sadie Brandt. And spending time with her. But no matter what happened later that evening, he was leaving town in the morning. That is, unless something turned up . . .

He went back to his hotel, spent the time til supper in his room, then left the room at quarter to eight to meet Sadie. He walked to the Red Cactus, very aware of his surroundings. He knew no one was following him, but that didn't mean they weren't waiting on a roof or at a window. Luckily, he made it to the Cactus without a shot being fired.

The saloon was busier at that late hour. He elbowed himself a place at the bar and ordered a cold beer while he waited for Sadie.

"She'll be down any minute," the bartender said, setting the beer down. "Here's another one on the house."

"What'd I do to deserve this?" Clint asked, picking it up.

"I dunno," the man said. "Maybe it's what you're gonna do."

The bartender smiled and moved on down the bar.

Clint turned with the beer in his hand. He noticed now that there were two younger girls working the floor, wearing dresses that revealed plenty of leg and shoulders, some cleavage.

When Sadie appeared at the top of the stairs, she attracted many of the male eyes in the room. She wore a purple dress, still rather sedate for a saloon, but it clung to her body, showing off her curves.

She came down the stairs slowly, crossed the room and stopped in front of Clint.

"You look great," he told her.

"Thank you."

"I feel underdressed."

"You're fine," she said. "The place we're going is known for its food, not its ambience." She turned and waved to the bartender. "Lenny, you're closing up tonight."

"Yes, Ma'am," he said. "Enjoy your supper."

"And watch the girls," she advised him. "And I mean their hands."

"Yes, Ma'am."

She linked her arm in Clint's left one and they walked out of the saloon together.

Outside Clint asked, "What was that about the girl's hands?"

"Lenny keeps looking at their legs, and I think one of them may be palming some money."

"And he's not?"

"Lenny's honest," she said, "and a little dumb, when it comes to the girls. But if I call him on it, he'll watch them. But let's not talk about business."

"What does that leave us?"

She smiled and asked, "Can't you guess?"

Chapter Seventeen

Clint saw what Sadie meant about the place when they arrived. There was no fancy stenciling on the window, or over the door, just a crude sign that said HASTY'S PLACE.

"Hasty?" he asked.

"He's a friend of mine," she said. "I did the sign for him."

When they got inside, the aroma coming from the kitchen belied the image presented by the outside.

"This place smells great," Clint said, as they were seated.

"It's a combination of all of Hasty's dishes."

"Since this is your place," Clint said, "I'm going to let you order for both of us."

He had started to do that whenever someone invited him to supper, and so far it had turned out okay each time.

When the waiter came Sadie asked, "Do you have venison today, Eddie?"

"Yes, Ma'am."

"Then we'll have two venison dinners."

"Comin' right up."

"I'm sure you've had venison before," she said, "but not the way Hasty prepares it."

While they waited for their meals Sadie asked, "So tell me, do you think the person who put the price on your head is a man or a woman?"

"I can't even be sure of that," Clint said. "If it's the relative of someone I was forced to kill, it could be either."

"Forced to kill?" she asked.

"I don't usually try to kill someone unless they're trying to kill me."

"That's admirable, for a man with your reputation."

"Just because I'm good with a gun, and can beat most people to the draw, doesn't mean I want to."

"It's been my experience that men who are better at something than other men, want to show it off, no matter what it is."

"Maybe that's because you've seen most of them when they've had a few drinks."

"That's true enough," she said. "Drunks are always braggarts."

When the venison came, he saw that he had been right to let her order for them both.

"How is it?" she asked.

"I've never tasted it like this," Clint said. "What's the secret?"

"That's just it," she said. "All of Hasty's recipes are secret. He doesn't tell anyone how he does it."

Over an excellent dessert of strawberry shortcake Clint said, "So your only interest in this place is that you painted the sign?"

"You got me," she said. "I'm also an investor."

"So you own the Cactus and a piece of this place," he said. "Anything else?"

"No, that's it," she said.

He looked around at all the occupied tables.

"Seems to me you're doing pretty well with both your businesses."

"I'm actually just where I want to be," she said, then added, "businesswise."

"What about moving to a larger city?" he asked. "Kansas City? Maybe Denver?"

"I've been to Denver," she said. "Don't like it."

"What's wrong with Denver?"

"Too crowded," she said. "As a matter of fact, the same is true of Kansas City, and St. Louis. And don't get me started on Chicago or New York. No, this town is just the right size for me—and it's slowly growing."

After supper they walked outside. The weather was cool, and pleasant.

"Would you walk me home?" she asked.

"It would be my pleasure," he said, "but perhaps, with someone out there trying to kill me, it wouldn't be a good idea."

She linked her arm into his left and said, "I'm willing to take the risk."

They started walking.

"Don't you want to go back to the Cactus and check on your girls?" he asked.

"I can do that tomorrow," she told him. "Believe me, I'm not looking forward to firing one of them, but it may have to be done."

"If you catch them stealing, won't you turn them over to the sheriff?"

"No," she said, "I take care of my own business. He's got enough to do with looking after the town."

"That's very understanding of you," he said. "That's not been my experience."

"You've been a town lawman?"

"Many, *many* years ago," he said.

"Why did you give it up?"

"Because," he said, "business owners expect you to be at their beck-and-call."

She tightened her hold on his arm.

"What if I told you I expect you to be at my beck-and-call tonight?"

Chapter Eighteen

Sadie had a small, well-cared for house on a street filled with them.

"Something else I bought with my poker money," she said.

"That must've been some game," he said.

"It was a winner-take-all tournament," she said.

He went up the walk with her to the front door and waited while she unlocked it. Then she turned and faced him.

"I have a really nice wine inside," she said.

"I'm not much of a wine drinker."

"I wasn't really talking about wine," she said, and kissed him.

The kiss went on for a while in the doorway, and then she hooked her finger in his shirt and drew him inside, locking the door behind them.

From what Clint could see in the darkness, the house was neat and well furnished, but he only got a glimpse as she led him through to her bedroom. Once there, she kissed him again, then backed off and began to disrobe as he watched. Before long, strips of moonlight from the window played across the naked curves of her body.

"Now you, please," she said. "I want to watch."

Clint shrugged and started with his gun, which he laid nearby. Then he proceeded to remove his boots, and his clothes, until he, too, was naked.

"Well, well," she said.

"Is that good?" he asked.

"You tell me."

"From where I'm standing," he said, "it's very good."

She stepped forward, took his hands in hers and tugged him to the bed.

"You interested me from the moment I saw you," she told him, "but I didn't plan to do this so soon, until you told me you were leaving."

"Well," he said, "I'm sorry I ruined your timetable."

She slid onto the bed, got under the sheet and said, "Oh, shut up and get in here."

He slid onto the bed with her, got under the sheet and she pressed herself to him, enveloping him in hot, smooth flesh. Their legs intertwined as they kissed, and then their hands began to roam. He ended up with her butt in his hands, and she took hold of his hardening cock.

"Ooh, this is nice," she said, stroking him.

"I couldn't agree more," he said, squeezing her ass cheeks.

They kissed again, and then Clint ran his mouth down to her neck, shoulders and breasts. She settled onto her back so he could easily continue down her body, kissing his way to the apex of her thighs where she was already wet.

He slid down and settled between her outstretched thighs, tended to her needs with his lips and tongue until a shudder ran through her thighs. Her entire body tensed, and then eased as she let out a long, animal-like growl . . .

***

"I wanted to scream," she told him, later, "but I'm not a screamer."

"Either way is fine with me," he said, as they lay side-by-side.

"Can I ask you something personal?"

"Sure, why not?" he said. "What we just did was real personal."

"You've been with a lot of women over the years, right?"

"I suppose you could say a lot, yeah."

"Do you think you ever left someone behind, like you're going to do to me, who hates you for it."

"Now hold on—"

"No, no," she said, "I'm not complaining. I know exactly what this was, and I have no complaints. I'm just wondering if other women felt. . . different."

"You're thinking that some woman I was with and left has put a price on my head?" he said. "Okay, yes, I've been with a lot of women. So how the hell would I figure out who it was?"

"Well, give it some thought," she said. "Do you think a woman you were with, say, ten years ago would suddenly decide to do that?"

"Probably not."

"So then maybe it's a woman you were with recently," she said. "Can you think of any who were upset with you for leaving?"

"I'm pretty sure the women I've been with have thought about it the way you are," Clint said. "I've never made any promises to anyone."

"I'm just trying to help you figure this out," she said.

"I'll have to do a lot of thinking if I go to South Dakota and find out nothing," he said. "I'll keep what you've said in mind."

"And now," she said, "I think I need to give you something else to think about, as well."

She closed her hand over his semi-hard cock, which started to stiffen again immediately. She stroked it until it was good and hard, and then took it into her mouth.

She was right. It was going to be something he remembered for a long time.

Chapter Nineteen

Clint stayed the entire night and left early the next morning. He thought about waking Sadie up as he slipped out but doubted she would be putting a price on his head if he didn't.

As he walked back to his hotel, he wondered about what Sadie had said. If it was a woman behind the bounty on his head, it made sense that it was someone he had been with recently. But he still thought he should concentrate on families of men he killed. And if a woman was behind this, it could possibly be a wife or a mother—or even a daughter.

The names he'd had in mind when he went to Kansas City wouldn't qualify. The two men were just business-men who didn't like him because he didn't like them. He had refused to work for them. They wouldn't have him killed for that. The woman he considered was a mean-spirited shrew he'd crossed swords with because her son tried to kill him. He didn't kill the boy, and she had appreciated it at the time, in her own way. Now none of those three people seemed to be in Kansas.

When he entered the hotel, the desk clerk waved him down.

"The sheriff was lookin' for you this mornin', Mr. Adams," the man said. "Told me to ask you to come by his office."

"I'll do that after breakfast," Clint said. "Thanks."

He went to his room first, to wash up and change into a clean shirt, then to a small café a few doors away for breakfast. When he finished eating, he would have gone to the livery for his Tobiano, but instead he walked to the sheriff's office.

" 'mornin'," Redmann said from behind his desk. "I know you said you were leavin' today, but I thought I'd catch you before you went."

"What's on your mind?"

"I need a favor," Redmann said, "and you have no reason to give it to me, but I recently lost my deputy and I need some help."

"If you're offering me a job, I can't—"

"No job," Redmann said, holding up his hand, "just a favor."

"What is it?"

"There are three varmints I want to get rid of," Redmann said. "I'm gonna order them out of town today, but I need some backup. You probably won't even have to use your gun. Just watch my back."

"When do you want to do this?" Clint asked.

"Well . . . now would be good."

"Do you know where they are now?" Clint asked.

"I definitely know where they are," Redmann said.

"Then let's get it done so I can be on my way."

"Excellent!" Redmann said, springing up from his desk.

***

As they approached a large, two story, yellow-sided building, Clint had an idea what it was.

"Whorehouse?" he asked.

"Good guess," Redmann said. "The only one we got in town. The Yellow Rose."

"Why not wait until they come out?" Clint asked.

"That's what I was gonna do," Redmann said, "but I'm not as young as I used to be, and if I did that, I'd have to face them alone. Three against one, you think they're gonna buck those odds?"

"Probably not. Do you know these fellas?"

"I do," Redmann said. "I've dealt with them before. Last time they were here I told them not to come back. Now I've gotta enforce that."

Clint could see the lawman's point. Why not make use of him while he was there. After all, Redmann had gone to the bank with him to talk to the manager. Clint felt he was simply returning the favor.

They mounted the porch and Redmann knocked on the front door. It was opened by a young redhead in a filmy nightgown. She had small breasts, but her nipples were very prominent, as were her freckles.

"Sheriff," she greeted. "Finally decide to sample our wares? And you brought a friend!"

"Very funny, Joy," Redmann said. "I need to see Mandy Rose."

"I'll tell 'er," Joy said, and withdrew, closing the door.

"Mandy Rose runs the Yellow Rose?" Clint asked.

"Not her real name," Redmann said.

When the door reopened, an older woman with a streak of grey in her black hair smiled at Redmann with her hand on her ample hip. Mandy Rose had obviously been a lovely young woman, but the wear-and-tear of her profession was showing, although there was still plenty of sexiness there.

"Jack!" she said. "What brings you here?"

"Are Linell and the others still here, Mandy?" Redmann asked.

"Yeah, they're all upstairs with girls. I expect Leah, Sutton and Ramona to show some bruises when it's all over."

"Well," Redmann said, "maybe I can keep that from happenin'."

"Be my guest," she said, standing aside to allow them to enter.

Chapter Twenty

Clint followed Sheriff Redmann down a hall and up a flight of stars. The lawman seemed to know his way around. They went down another hall and stopped in front of a door.

"I don't know which one of them is in here, but whoever it is will deliver the message."

Redmann opened the door and stepped in, followed by Clint, who saw a big, pale, naked, pock-marked butt.

"Daniels!" Redmann snapped.

The owner of the butt suddenly turned, his eyes wide, and then got off the woman he'd been straddling.

"Sheriff!" he said. "You scared me."

"Get off the bed, Daniels, and the girl."

Daniels did as he was told, and Clint got a look at a thin, frail looking blonde.

"Okay, Sutton," Redmann said, "out."

"Yes, Sir." She jumped out of bed, grabbed her nightgown, held it over herself and ran from the room.

"Aw now, Sheriff, a man's gotta finish what he started," the sallow looking youth whined.

"Not today, Daniels," Redmann said. "Get your friends and meet me outside, now."

Redmann didn't wait for a reply.

"You think they'll come out?" Clint asked, as they went down the stairs.

"They'll come out," Redmann said. "When Daniels tells Linell I'm here, he'll wanna face me."

They passed several girls along the way to the front door, and then stepped outside.

"And who's Linell?"

"If they have a leader, he's it," Redmann said.

"This Daniels looks like a kid," Clint said. "Are they all that young?"

"They're young, and mean," Redmann said. "This town doesn't need their kind."

When the three men appeared at the front door and stepped out onto the porch, Clint saw that they were all in their early twenties. While Daniels was sickly thin, the other two seemed healthy enough. One of them had an arrogant smirk on his face. Clint was willing to bet this was Linell.

"Sheriff Redmann," Linell said, as they came down the stairs. "What's so important that you had to interrupt our pleasures?"

All three of the young men wore holstered pistols.

"Sheriff," Linell said, as they came down the steps, "last time we were here I felt bad for you and let you run us out of town. That ain't gonna happen this time, not even if you got a new deputy."

"This man's not my deputy," Redmann said. "He's just a friend."

"So what's your friend doin' here?"

"Just backin' me up," Redmann said.

Clint was impressed that Redmann was not using Clint's reputation by telling them his name. But Linell wouldn't let it go.

"So what's your name, friend?" Linell asked Clint.

"Do you really want to know?" Clint asked.

Linell laughed.

"Don't tell me you're shy."

"People don't always react well to hearing my name," Clint told him.

"I think I'll take a chance."

"Clint Adams."

Linell stared at him, then started laughing.

"Why is that funny?" the sheriff asked.

"Why not say Wild Bill Hickok?" Linell asked.

"Wild Bill is dead," Clint said. "I'm not."

Linell stopped laughing and stared at Clint. The other two young men began to fidget.

"Sheriff . . ." Linell said.

"He's tellin' the truth," Redmann said. "He's Clint Adams."

"What's the Gunsmith doin' in a town like Windham?" Linell asked.

"Passing through," Clint said.

"Then why are you here," Linell said, "now?"

"Like the sheriff said, I'm just helping out," Clint replied.

Linell looked at Redmann.

"Time to leave, Linell," the lawman said. "And don't come back."

"Oh, we'll be back," Linell said, pointing his finger at Redmann. "And next time you won't have the Gunsmith backin' your play."

As Linell and the other two turned to walk away, Clint said to Redmann, "He's right, you know. Next time you won't have backup. So I suggest we get this done now."

All three of the young men turned back.

"What?" Linell said.

"You heard me," Clint said. "Go for your guns, boys."

"What?" Daniels said.

"Now wait—" Linell said, holding out his hands.

"Either go for your guns now," Clint said, "or leave and never come back. If I hear you did, and anything happens to the sheriff, I'll be back. I'll find you all, and we'll finish this. Understood?"

The three men stared at him, then Linell said, "Yeah, we understand."

"Then go!"

The three of them turned and hurried away.

Sheriff Redmann looked at Clint.

"Well," he said, "that didn't go quite the way I thought it would. I appreciate that last part."

"It remains to be seen if they stay away," Clint said. "Linell was right, I won't be around next time."

"Don't worry," Redmann said. "I'll soon have a couple of deputies. All I need is for the Town Council to approve the budget."

"Well, I hope they do," Clint said.

"Come on," Redmann said, "I'll walk to the livery stable with you."

"Why do I feel like you just want to make sure I leave town, too?" Clint asked.

Redmann smiled and said, "I hope you find what you're lookin' for."

***

J.B. Patrick looked up from his desk as his assistant, Edward McNee, entered his office, holding a yellow slip of paper.

"What is it?" he asked.

"It's Clint Adams, Sir," McNee said.

Patrick abandoned the business on his desk. This took precedence over everything else.

"What've you got?"

"A telegram from Windham, Kansas."

"What's it say?"

McNee held it up to read.

"Don't read it to me!" Patrick snapped. "Just tell me what it says."

"Yes, Sir," McNee replied. "It says Adams was there, but now he's on his way to Windham, South Dakota."

"Excellent!" Patrick said. He grabbed a cigar from the box on his desk and lit it, puffed on it contentedly.

"What should I do, Sir?"

"Send every hired gun we have to Windham, South Dakota," Patrick said. "I'm tired of pussyfooting around. Raise the price on the Gunsmith's head to two thousand dollars."

"Yes, Sir."

"And get me a train ticket."

"To where, sir?"

"The nearest stop to Windham," Patrick said. "From there get me a buggy and a driver."

"Yes, Sir."

"And McNee."

"Yes, Sir?"

"Get me a driver who can use a gun."

Chapter Twenty-One

When Clint bypassed Deadwood on his way to Windham, South Dakota, it brought back unwanted memories of the cowardly murder of his friend, Wild Bill Hickok. It happened years ago, but sometimes the pain felt as fresh as ever. Not only did he lose a friend, but now he felt he was probably going to die the same way—from a bullet. He was just determined that it wouldn't be a coward's bullet, like the one that killed Bill. No, if and when he was killed by a bullet, it would be one fired by a better gun than him.

Leaving Deadwood behind, he rode on to the town of Windham, South Dakota. He had never been there before. In fact, he had never heard of it before seeing the name on the bottom of that wanted poster. He had no idea what to expect, but when he rode in and found that it was a small town, he wasn't surprised.

One of the first things he spotted as he rode down Windham's main street was a poster nailed to a wall. He rode the Tobiano over so he could read it. It was the same poster he had folded up in his pocket, only this one said the price was two thousand, not one.

The price on the Gunsmith's head had doubled.

Clint thought he should stop in first to see the town sheriff. With that price there was bound to be trouble. He found the office, dismounted, tied off the Tobiano and went to the door. As he entered, two men turned and looked at him, both wearing badges. One was old, one was young. He made the mistake of assuming the older one was the sheriff.

"Sheriff?"

"That's right," the young man said, "Sheriff Thad Turner. This is my deputy, Liam."

The deputy nodded.

"What can we do for you, stranger?" the sheriff asked.

"I just thought I'd stop in and let you know I was in town."

"And why would you do that?" Turner asked.

"Sheriff," the deputy said, "this is Clint Adams."

The sheriff looked surprised.

"What the hell is the Gunsmith doin' here?" the lawman asked.

"There's a bit of a story behind that," Clint admitted. "You've seen the posters?"

"Two thousand dollars for the Gunsmith, dead?" Turner said. "You mean that's on the level?"

"It's not an official wanted poster," Clint said, "but yes, somebody's putting up that money."

"Because you're the Gunsmith?" the deputy asked. "Or is it more personal?"

"That's what I'm here to find out," Clint said.

"What makes you think your answer is here?" the deputy asked.

"Apparently, the money is being held in the Bank of Windham."

"How do you know that?" Sheriff Turner asked.

"It says so at the bottom of the poster."

"So somebody is setting up my town to be a shootin' gallery?"

"Looks like it."

"That explains a lot," the deputy said.

"What do you mean?" Clint asked.

"We were wonderin' what all these gunnies are doin' in town," the deputy said. "Apparently, they're waitin' for you."

"How many are we talking about?" Clint asked.

"Half a dozen, so far," Turner said.

"Are they together?"

"No," the deputy said, "they each rode in separate, and they've stayed that way. My guess is, they're gonna be competin' for the money."

"Maybe," Sheriff Turner said, "you should just turn around and ride out."

"I'm afraid I can't do that."

"That's what I thought you'd say."

Chapter Twenty-Two

Clint left the sheriff's office and went directly to one of Windham's two hotels, The Gregory Hotel.

"And how long will you be staying with us, Sir?" the young clerk asked.

"Probably longer than I want to," Clint said.

"Sir?" The clerk frowned.

"Sorry," Clint said. "I'm not sure, but probably a few days."

The clerk handed him his key and he went up to his room. It overlooked the main street, but there was no access from outside, and the buildings across the street were only one story, so it was acceptable.

He stayed in the room only long enough to drop off his rifle and saddlebags, then left intending to go to the bank. But when he got to the lobby he saw the deputy, Liam, waiting there.

"I thought we should talk," the older man said.

"The sheriff send you over?"

"He doesn't know I'm here."

"Then why *are* you here?"

"He's not just the sheriff," Liam said, "he's my son."

A Price on a Gunsmith's Head

***

Deputy Liam Turner took Clint to a café near the hotel.

"Don't wanna go to a saloon," he explained. "Might run into one of those hired guns."

"That's going to happen sooner or later," Clint figured. "I just hope I can get one of them to tell me who put the price on my head."

They went to a rear table and had a coffee each.

"Nothin' else, Liam?" the middle-aged waitress asked.

"No, Gina," he said. "Coffee's enough."

The waitress nodded and walked away.

"So," Clint asked, "what's this about?"

"I was sheriff here for many years," Liam said. "Recently, I stepped down, and my kid stepped up."

"Then why are you a deputy?"

"To help him out, get him settled," Liam said. "He's got a lot to learn."

"Okay," Clint said, "but that still doesn't tell me why we're here."

"I don't want Thad gettin' between you and your shooters," Liam said.

"And how do we avoid that?"

"By you leavin' town."

"How else?"

Liam shrugged.

"That's it," he said. "You hafta go."

"I told you and the sheriff, I can't do that."

"I know what you told us," Deputy Turner said. "How do I get you to leave without forcin' you?"

"I can only think of one way."

"And how's that?"

"Tell me who put the price on my head."

"I don't know," the deputy said.

"Well, as soon as I find out, I'll leave."

Deputy Liam Turner sipped his coffee.

"I didn't want to bring this up," he said, "but I'm a pretty fast gun, myself."

"Good for you," Clint said. "You'll be real useful to your son."

"Adams—"

"Look," Clint said, "I'm going to talk to the bank manager. If he tells me what I want to know, I'm gone."

"And if these gunnies decide to try you, one at a time?" Liam asked.

"That'll be their hard luck," Clint said.

Chapter Twenty-Three

"If it looks like my kid is gonna get between you and one of the shooters, I'll be there," he told Clint, outside the café.

"I understand, Deputy," Clint said. "I'm hoping it won't come to that."

"I know your reputation, Adams," the deputy said, "and I ain't afraid of it, so you better hope it don't."

Clint watched the old lawman walk away and had the feeling the man would be formidable in a gunfight. He wasn't looking forward to finding out.

***

The bank surprised him.

It was small and didn't look like an establishment that would even have two thousand dollars on deposit. Another surprise came when he asked the one teller if the manager was around.

"Yes, Sir," the young teller said, "that would be me."

"You're the bank manager?"

"Yes, Sir."

"How old are you?"

"Twenty-five."

"Is there some sort of youth movement going on in this town?"

"Sir?"

"I met your sheriff."

"Oh, I see," the teller/manager said. "I suppose you might say that."

"How old is your mayor?"

"I'm not sure," the young man said, "but he's over forty."

"What's your name?" Clint asked.

"Russell Grimes, Sir," the bank manager said. "Can I help you open an account?"

"I'm not here to open an account."

"Then what can I do for you?"

Clint took the poster from his pocket and unfolded it. He slid it across to Grimes.

"What do you know about this?"

Grimes picked it up, looked at it, and went pale.

"Sir," he asked, "did you kill Clint Adams?"

"No," Clint said, "I *am* Clint Adams."

If possible, Grimes went even paler.

"Um . . ."

"Relax, son," Clint said. "I want to know who issued this poster."

"Um, I don't know, Sir."

"But you know about it."

"Yes, Sir."

"And you have the money in your bank?"

"Y-yes, Sir."

"And you'll play it to whoever kills me?"

"Well, Sir . . . they would have to prove that they killed you."

Clint took the poster back.

"How can you not know who put the money in your bank?" he asked.

"At the time," Grimes said, "I wasn't the manager."

"Who was?"

"Mr. Dixon."

"And where do I find him?"

"The cemetery."

"How did he die?"

"He had a heart attack."

"But if someone comes in and can prove they killed me, you'll pay them?"

"Yes, Sir."

"Come on, Mr. Grimes," Clint said. "It's got to be written down somewhere who deposited that money. Who put out this poster?"

"Mr. Dixon had the papers," Grimes said. "I don't know where they are."

"Then how do you know you have to pay it off?" Clint asked.

"Mr. Dixon told me so," Grimes said.

"So you only have his word," Clint said. "You've got nothing in writing?"

"That's right."

"Then why would you do it?"

"Because Mr. Dixon was the bank manager," Grimes said. "He hired me, he taught me. I owe him."

"All right," Clint said, "but do me a favor, will you?"

"If I can."

"Look around," Clint said, "see if you find anything in writing."

The young bank manager nodded.

"I'll do that, Mr. Adams."

"Thanks."

Clint turned and left the bank. As he came out the front door, he saw two men in their thirties, standing in the street, facing the bank. They both wore guns. It didn't take a genius to know what they were doing there.

Chapter Twenty-Four

"Clint Adams!" one of them shouted.

"That's right."

"Nothin' personal," the man said, "but there's two thousand dollars on your head."

"You wouldn't happen to know who put it there, would you?" Clint asked.

"No," the man said, "All we know is if we kill you, we go in that bank and get paid."

"How do you know that?"

The man shrugged.

"The word's out," he said.

The other man spoke for the first time.

"You don't know who wants you dead enough to pay two thousand dollars?" he asked in disbelief.

"No, I don't."

"I wish we could help ya," the first man said. "I mean, a man oughtta know why he's dyin'."

"I agree," Clint said. "You two are dying for two thousand dollars that you'll never see."

The men stood about six feet apart, showing that they knew what they were doing.

"Well, Adams," the first man said, "we gotta try."

"I guess I can't fault you for that," Clint said. "Go ahead."

The two tensed, which was the tell that they were about to draw. They knew what they were doing, but that tell was uncontrollable. If he had been facing one man, Clint might have been able to get fancy, but with two foes facing him, he had no choice. He drew quickly, fired twice, hitting both men in the chest. One fell over backward, while the other simply slumped like a puppet whose strings had been cut.

Clint stepped into the street, reloading as he walked. Townspeople who hadn't ducked inside for safety, stopped to stare. And running down the street toward him were both lawmen, the father and son, sheriff and deputy.

"What the hell—" Sheriff Turner snapped, as both men came to a halt.

"Looks like it's started," Deputy Turner said, studying the dead men.

"Do you know them?" Clint asked.

"Bob Melvin and Brett Hugo. Two locals. They're far from the worst of the bunch that are here, waitin' for you."

"I could see that," Clint said.

"I'm gonna get some men to move the bodies," the sheriff said. "Should take about half an hour. Be in my office when I get there."

"Sure, Sheriff," Clint said.

Tuner looked at his deputy.

"Stay here til I get some men."

"Sure, Sheriff."

Turner looked at Clint, then turned and walked away.

"One shot each, huh?" Deputy Turner said. "Clean?"

"They knew what they were doing," Clint said, "but they weren't good enough to get it done."

"They're just the first," Turner said.

"I know."

The deputy looked at the bank.

"Find out anythin' in there?"

"You knew I wouldn't," Clint said. "This town's got a young sheriff and a young bank manager."

"Yeah," Deputy Turner said, "things are changin' around here. The town's gonna grow, but first we have to get rid of you and your trouble."

"Then help me," Clint said. "Tell me who put the price on my head, and I'll go."

"I'll see what I can find out," Turner said. "Meanwhile, you better get over to the sheriff's office."

"Yes, I better."

***

Clint was sitting at the sheriff's desk when the young lawman walked in.

"Do you mind?" the sheriff asked.

Clint stood up and moved.

"You need another chair."

Sheriff Turner sat down.

"That would encourage visitors," he said.

"What about for your deputy?"

The sheriff almost smiled.

"He usually parks his hip on my desk."

Clint did the same thing.

"What can I do for you, Sheriff?"

"You can leave town."

"As soon as I find out what I came to find out," Clint said. "That's a promise."

"And can you promise not to kill anyone else on my streets?" Sheriff Turner asked.

"I can only promise that I'm going to defend myself," Clint said.

The sheriff regarded him for a few more moments, then waved a hand and said, "Get out."

"I'm not looking for trouble, Sheriff," Clint said. "I'm actually looking to prevent it."

"Sure," the sheriff said. "I get it. Just do me a favor and try to get your information as soon as possible."

Clint stood up straight.

"That's my plan," he said, and left the office.

Chapter Twenty-Five

As Clint left the sheriff's office, Deputy Turner was approaching.

"He tell you to leave town?" Turner asked.

"He did."

"But you ain't, are you?"

"No, I'm not."

"Look, I talked with Grimes at the bank," the deputy said. "He pretty much told me what he told you."

"What about the older bank manager, Dixon? Where are his personal effects?"

"Gone," the deputy said. "He died months ago."

"How many months?"

Turner thought a moment, then said. "Three."

"So the price was put on my head before he died," Clint said. "Why has it taken three months for the attempts on my life to start?"

"Maybe," Deputy Turner said, "whoever put the price on your head was in prison."

"He could've had somebody deposit the money for him while he was inside."

"But maybe he didn't want you killed until he got out," Turner said. "So he could see it."

"Well, that's something I never thought about," Clint said. "Somebody I put in prison. Thanks, Deputy. Is there a telegraph office in town?"

"No."

"Where's the nearest one?"

"That would be Deadwood."

Deadwood. The last place Clint wanted to go.

***

Remembering what Deputy Turner had said about going to a saloon, Clint went to the café Turner had taken him to for coffee.

"Are ya meetin' Liam here?" Gina asked.

"No," Clint said, "this time it's just me."

"What can I get ya?"

"Do you serve beer?" he asked.

"We do," she said, "but it'd be cheaper at one of the saloons."

"That's okay," he said. "I'll have a beer."

"You hungry?" Gina asked. "It'd be cheaper with somethin' to eat."

"That's a good idea," he said. "Bring me a sandwich."

"What kind?"

"Surprise me," he said. "Something that goes good with beer."

"Comin' up."

While he waited, he looked around. Most of the tables were empty. A couple of them were occupied by families with children, all of whom were finding him very interesting. The mothers seemed to be urging the fathers to pay their check so they could leave. By the time the waitress came out of the kitchen only one other table was occupied, by a single man who was concentrating on his lunch.

She set a plate and a beer down in front of Clint and said, "Beer goes with steak, so you've got yourself a steak sandwich."

"Thank you."

She looked around and said, "So much for the lunch rush." Then returned to the kitchen.

Clint went to work on his sandwich, washing it down with sips of cold beer. It was fairly obvious to him, after being forced to kill the two locals, that the gunmen who came after him for the two thousand dollars had no way of knowing who put the price on his head. And if they didn't know, and the bank that was holding the money didn't know, then who did?

***

He finished his sandwich and beer, paid the waitress and thanked her with a generous tip.

"Tell Liam I said hi," she told him as he started to leave.

"You like him, don't you?" Clint asked.

The place was empty now except for the two of them, so she paused before going back to the kitchen.

"I've known him a long time."

"When he was sheriff?"

"And before," she said.

"Did you know his wife?"

"Yes, we were friends."

"Then you also know his son, the sheriff?" Clint asked.

She laughed and said, "Since he was a pup. When his mother died, I tried to help raise him."

"How did she die?"

"A fever," she said. "The doc's not even sure what it was, but it took her quick."

"What do you think of them as lawmen?" Clint asked.

"Liam was a great sheriff," she said. "He only stepped down because he knew Thad wanted to follow in his footsteps. He'll make Thad a good lawman, as well."

"So they're honest?"

"As the day is long," she said.

"Thank you for talking to me."

"Are you Clint Adams?" she asked, as he headed for the door. "The man who killed the two local gunmen this mornin'?"

"I'm afraid so," he said.

"Those boys deserved what they got," she told him, "but I hope you ain't here to make trouble for Liam and Thad."

"Believe it or not, Ma'am," Clint said, "I'm here to try and avoid trouble."

"Well then, you're welcome to come back here and eat any time."

"Thanks," he said. "I'll keep that in mind."

Chapter Twenty-Six

Clint was still finding it hard to believe that the young bank manager knew nothing about the two-thousand-dollar deposit. But he also found that he had some respect for Deputy Liam Turner, and the deputy seemed to believe Grimes.

After leaving the café, Clint thought that perhaps it was time to go to one of the saloons. There was no point in avoiding them. Anybody who wanted to find him would have no trouble anyway. And walking into a saloon and having a beer would show that he wasn't worried.

There were two saloons in town, The Bent Tree and The War Wagon. From the outside they seemed to be equal, so he chose The War Wagon.

As he entered, he was immediately aware of the attention he attracted. He might have thought it was because he was a stranger in town, but after what had happened outside the bank, he doubted that was the case. Almost everybody in town must have heard who he was by now.

The place was about half full, but as he approached the bar, patrons picked up their drinks and moved. Nobody wanted to be near him if shooting started again.

"Beer, please," he said to the bartender, a fortyish, very nervous looking man. Clint was amazed he managed to serve the beer without spilling it.

"Thanks."

"S-sure, Mr. Adams."

Clint looked around the room, trying to pick out the gunmen. It wasn't hard. They all had the look, and they were all staring at him. In addition, they were sitting at their own tables. Professional guns had no desire to share bounty money, unlike the two young men that morning.

Quite a few of the patrons of The War Wagon Saloon decided it was time to leave. This left Clint alone with virtually every gunman in town. He decided to take advantage of the opportunity.

He finished his beer, set the mug down on the bar with a loud bang, then did it two more times.

"I don't know any of you," he announced, "but you apparently all know who I am."

There were five of them, and they looked around at each other.

"And maybe you don't even know each other," Clint said. "No matter. I killed two men this morning who tried to collect the price on my head. If any of you intend to try and collect, keep that in mind." He turned to the bartender. "Give each of these men a drink, on me." Then back to the men. "If I were you, I'd drink it up and leave town. If you don't leave, then you better draw straws to see in what order you'll face me." He put money on the bar to pay for the drinks. "Or, in what order you'll die."

He turned and left the saloon.

***

After Clint left the saloon and the five men had their free drinks, one said, "Who's he think he's kiddin'?"

"Whataya mean?" another asked.

"Buyin' us drinks and talkin' to us like that," the man said. "I ain't leavin' town without taking a shot at that two thousand dollars."

"Not before I do," another man said.

"Now wait," still another said, "he had a good idea."

"What idea?"

"About drawin' straws to see who goes first," the man said.

The five men exchanged glances, and one said, "I suppose that's better than us shootin' it out to see who gets 'im."

They all laughed.

"Bartender!" one shouted. "Do you have straws?"

"Um, no, Sir," the bartender said, "but I've got some matches."

"Lucifers?"

"Yes, Sir."

"Good," the man said, "take five of the sticks and break them into five lengths. Then you'll hold them, and we'll all draw. Long match goes first, and so on."

The fifth man, who hadn't spoken yet, said, "I don't suppose any of us wants to team up and split the money after we kill 'im?"

They all looked around again, then started laughing.

"Come on, barkeep," one said, "get those matches."

***

Clint watched the action from outside through the window. He could see and hear everything, but they couldn't see him. He was hoping they might have discussed who had placed the price on his head, but they were only concerned with getting their try at the money, not with who was paying it.

Clint wondered what the five men's names were, but he probably would find that out, one-by-one, after he killed them. As they set about drawing matches from the bartender's hand, Clint turned and walked away.

Chapter Twenty-Seven

Clint saw Deputy Turner coming out of the sheriff's office and crossed over to intercept him.

"I just came from The War Wagon Saloon," he told the deputy.

"No shots fired?"

"Not yet," Clint said. "They're drawing straws to see who goes first."

Turner started to laugh, then stopped.

"You're serious?"

"Dead serious."

"How many of them were in there?" Turner asked.

"Five."

"That means there's probably three more at the Bent Tree," Turner said.

"Eight?" Clint asked. "So there were ten, until . . ."

"Until you killed the two locals," Turner said.

"Yes."

"You know what?" Turner said. "I'll go to the War Wagon and see what I can do."

"Like what?"

Turner shrugged.

"Take the straws away from them."

"You're not going over there alone, are you?" Clint asked. "You'll take the sheriff with you?"

Turner looked over his shoulder at the door of the sheriff's office.

"Naw," he said, "I'm just gonna talk to 'em."

"You saw them all ride into town?" Clint asked.

"One at a time, yeah," Turner said.

"You know who any of them are?"

"Not by name," Turner said, "but I know 'em. I've dealt with their kind for forty years."

"Are you sure you should walk into that saloon alone, Deputy?"

"You did, didn't you?" Turner asked. "And you're the one they want. If they didn't all draw their guns and shoot you down for two thousand dollars, they ain't gonna do it to me for nothin'."

"That makes sense," Clint said, "but still . . ."

"Relax, Adams," Turner said, "I've done this many times before."

"Maybe I should come with you anyway."

"Now that might start some shootin'," Turner said. "Just let me flash my badge and see if I can talk some sense into any of them."

"I gave them a chance to walk away," Clint said.

"From two thousand dollars?" Turner said. "I'd be lyin' if I said I wasn't tempted, myself."

"Deputy—"

"I'm kiddin'!" Turner said. "Look, stay away from the saloons until I come for you. Okay?"

"Sure."

As Turner started away Clint said, "Oh, one more thing, Deputy."

"What's that?"

"The waitress at the café said to tell you hello."

Turner waved and kept going.

***

Over the next hour or so there were no shots. Clint felt fairly sure the deputy was safe, but he would have liked to be a fly on the wall when the man walked into The War Wagon.

There was a knock on the door of his room, and he answered it, thinking it would be Deputy Turner. Instead, it was Sheriff Turner. No sooner had he opened the door than the young man punched him in the face. Clint staggered back, almost drawing his gun until he saw who it was.

"What the hell, Sheriff—"

"You're comin' with me."

"Where?" Clint asked, rubbing his jaw. "And what for?"

112

"The War Wagon."

"What happened?"

"You sent my father in there alone to do your dirty work," Turner said.

"That was his idea," Clint said. "I offered to go with him, and he refused."

"Did he say what he intended to do?"

"He said he was going to flash his badge and see if he could talk some sense into them. Why? What happened? Is he all right?"

"He's over at Doc's with some busted ribs, cuts and bruises. Those five gun toughs sittin' in that saloon beat the hell out of him when they saw his badge."

"So what do you intend to do about it?"

"I'm goin' over there to show them my badge," Sheriff Turner said. "Only this time you're comin' with me."

"What for, exactly?"

"I'm arrestin' the lot of them," Turner said, "and I just might let you kill one or two."

Chapter Twenty-Eight

Clint did not expect to be back at The War Wagon so soon, but he felt bad about what had happened to Deputy Turner. So he agreed to go with Sheriff Turner.

As they entered, Clint noticed some of the regular patrons had returned, but now they all turned and looked at Turner and Clint.

"Get out," the sheriff said. "All you regulars . . . out!"

The men made quickly for the door, leaving only the five gunmen, still seated at separate tables.

"What's on your mind, Sheriff?" one of them asked.

"My deputy was in here earlier," Turner said. "Seems some of you decided he needed to be taught a lesson. Now I think it's your turn."

"Is that a fact?"

"No," the sheriff said, "the fact is you're all under arrest for assaulting my deputy. Stand up!"

They all looked around at each other, and then the spokesman said, "Are you sure you want to do this, Sheriff? I mean, after all, your deputy just got a few bruises."

"And some broken ribs," Sheriff Turner said. "Now I want you all to take your guns out and put them on the table in front of you. Once that's done, we're gonna walk over to the jail."

All five men stood up, but none of them placed their guns on the table.

"Sheriff, we didn't know each other when we came to town. But right now, I don't think any of the five of us wanna go to jail."

"Why not?" Clint asked. "It's a simple assault charge. You'll probably have to pay a fine after a few days."

"Meanwhile," the man said, "somebody else kills you and gets the two thousand." He looked at Thad Turner. "Maybe you, Sheriff?"

"I don't have any interest in that money," Turner said. "The fact is, Adams is right. You'll probably be out in a few days. If you don't come along, you might just end up dead right here and now."

"You'd kill us for roughing up your old deputy?" the man asked.

"I'd kill you for puttin' your hands on my old man."

"Your old—what?"

"My father," Turner said. "The deputy is also my father. Get it?"

"It was his idea," one of the other men said, pointing to the spokesman.

"Shut up!" the man said. "We all did it."

"What's your name?" Turner asked.

"Del Webber."

"I never heard of you."

"You will," Webber said. "Some day."

The young sheriff impressed Clint with his next words.

"I tell you what I'll do," he said. "The other four of your ride out of town and don't come back. I'll put Mr. Webber here in a cell, since roughing up my deputy seems to have been his idea."

"It may've been my idea, but they all went along with it," Webber argued.

"Well, it looks like you're the one who's gonna have to pay for it. Whataya say, boys?"

"We keep our guns?" one of them asked.

"Take 'em with you when you leave," Turner said.

They considered the pitch for a few moments, then suddenly one of them walked to the door and left, followed by another.

"He's bluffin'!" Webber snapped "Come on!"

The third man shook his head and left.

The fourth man looked at Clint, who knew what he was thinking, that he'd like to try it. The two thousand dollars was almost within his grasp—but then he, too, made the right decision and left.

"How do you wanna play this, Webber?" Turner asked. "All of a sudden you have no advantage."

"Look, Sheriff," Webber said, "just step aside now and I'll take Adams and collect my money."

"If I do that, Adams will kill you," Turner said.

"And that would solve your problem. Wouldn't it?"

The young sheriff said, "That would actually give me a whole new problem to deal with. But right now you're my problem. Put your gun on the table and let's go."

"I don't think so, Sheriff," Webber said. "If you won't let me deal with Adams, I'll deal with you first, and then him."

Webber dropped his right hand down by his holster.

"Sheriff—" Clint started.

"Stay out of it, Adams," he said. "You did your job already."

Clint moved aside and stood at the bar, watching Webber closely. If the gunman killed the sheriff, he would have to face him next.

Only that turned out to not be the problem.

"You're lucky you didn't have to deal with my Pa's gun, Webber," Turner said.

"Yeah, why's that?"

"He's even faster than I am."

Turner didn't give Webber the first move, he simply drew and fired before the gunman could even clear leather.

Clint was impressed.

Chapter Twenty-Nine

As several men dropped the body of Webber into a wooden box at the undertaker's, Clint asked. "Where'd you learn to shoot like that?"

"You mean that fast," Turner asked, "or first?"

"Either one."

"Bein' fast comes natural," Turner said. "You should know that. My Pa is even faster. Shootin' first, I learned that from Pa. You don't give a man a chance to kill you if you don't have to."

"How old are you Sheriff?"

"I'm twenty-four."

"How many men have you killed?"

"Do you count?"

"No, I don't."

"Neither do I," Turner said. "That's somethin' else I learned from my Pa. You kill when you have to, and you don't keep count."

"That makes perfect sense."

"Potter's field, Sheriff?" the old undertaker asked.

"Yeah," Turner said, "the town will pay for it."

"Yes, Sir."

Sheriff Turner and Clint left the undertaker's office and started walking.

"Where are you headed?" Clint asked.

"Doc's," Turner said. "I wanna check on my Pa."

"Mind if I tag along?"

"No, I don't mind."

***

Doc Ted Wilson said Deputy Turner was going to be all right.

"I wrapped him real tight; his ribs may only be bruised, not broken," the old sawbones said. "The other cuts and bruises will heal. But he should take it easy for a while."

"I'll see that he does, Doc," Sheriff Turner said, "thanks."

They left the office with Liam Turner between them.

"Let's go home, Pa," Thad said.

"What happened to those men in the saloon?" the deputy asked.

"I ran them out of town," Thad told his father.

"Alone?"

"No," the young sheriff said, "I learned from you. I took Adams with me."

"What happened?"

"We ran four off, but the other—well, he's dead," Sheriff Turner said.

Deputy Turner looked at Clint.

"You?"

"No."

"I did it." Thad said. "He pushed it. I had no choice."

"That's the only time you kill, so—Sheriff," Deputy Turner said. "When you have no other choice."

"Can we go home now, Pa?" the sheriff asked.

Liam winced.

"We should go back to work," he said.

"I'll go back," the sheriff said, "as soon as I get you settled."

"Thad—"

"Don't argue with me, Deputy," Thad Turner said. "I'm your boss, remember?"

"I remember," Turner said.

"Thanks for the backup, Adams," the young sheriff said. "But don't forget, there are still a few money guns in town."

"I'll remember," Clint said.

"Try not to kill any of them, til I get back to town," Sheriff Turner said.

"Understood," Clint replied.

***

Over at The Bent Tree Saloon the word had gotten around not only about what Clint Adams had done, but what the sheriff just did. Unlike the five guns who were in the War Wagon, the three sitting in The Bent Tree knew each other.

"Sounds like somebody got rid of the competition for us," Reese Morton said.

"So that just leaves the three of us?" Vance Morton asked.

"Looks like it," Charlie Bennett said.

"Let's wait a while, give 'im a little more rope," Reese Morton proposed.

"Yeah, sure," his younger brother Vance said, "Ain't no hurry.

"Let him get a little more complacent—"

"Huh?" Vance asked.

"Relaxed," Reese explained, "let's wait until he's a little more relaxed."

"Why didn't you just say that?" Vance said, in disgust. "You don't have to make up words."

Reese looked across the table at his younger brother. Maybe some of this two thousand dollars should send the kid to school.

Chapter Thirty

Clint woke the next morning and went to the café for breakfast. As the waitress came to his table, he realized he didn't know her name.

"Gina," she said, when he asked her.

"Well, Gina, I said hello to Liam for you yesterday," Clint told her.

"I appreciate that."

"Yeah, it was right before he had to go to the doctor."

"He what?"

"The doctor," Clint said. "Oh, sorry, you didn't know?"

"Know what? Is he sick?"

"No, he got, uh, into it with a few fellas at The War Wagon."

"Did he get shot?"

"No, just roughed up, a bit," Clint said. "The sheriff took care of it, though."

"Thad?" she said. "Did he go after them alone, the fool boy?"

"Uh, no," Clint said, "I went with him."

"And then what happened?"

"He ran the men out of town."

"Wait . . . I heard there was a shootin'," she said. "Was that it?"

"Yes, that was it."

"Jesus!"

The other diners looked up from their table in surprise.

"Order your breakfast," she told him.

"Ham-and-eggs and coffee."

She turned and went to the kitchen. When she brought him his plate and coffee, she sat across from him.

"How bad?"

"What?"

"How bad was Liam hurt?"

He started to eat.

"Answer my questions and your breakfast is on the house," she said. "How bad?"

"Some bumps and bruises."

"Is that all?"

He hesitated, chewed, swallowed, drank some coffee. He should've kept his mouth shut or eaten breakfast someplace else.

"The doctor said he might have a couple of cracked ribs. But he'll be fine."

"The fool!" she said.

"Him or his son?" he asked.

"Both!" she swore. "One's an old fool and one's a young one. They're gonna get themselves killed."

"I thought you said they were good lawmen," Clint reminded her.

"I told you they were honest," she said. "Oh, Liam was good in his day, but his day is past."

"The young one looked pretty good to me," Clint said.

"He's just tryin' to be like his father," she said. "Liam went forty years without gettin' himself killed. You think the same is likely to be true of Thad?"

"There's always danger when you wear a badge or a gun," Clint said.

"Especially if you wear both," she added, shaking her head. "I'll just have to stop in and see him tonight." She stood up. "Enjoy your breakfast. I'll bring some biscuits and another pot of coffee."

"Thank you, Gina."

She returned to the kitchen and left him to eat in peace.

***

After breakfast Clint put a tip on the table for Gina and left the café. He headed toward the sheriff's office to see if Thad Turner was there. As he started across the street a shot was fired and a bullet struck the ground at his feet. Instinctively, he turned, drew and fired. His bullet struck the man on the roof, who dropped his rifle two stories to the ground. Then followed himself. People walking on the street scattered or stopped and stared as Clint walked to the fallen man.

Sheriff Turner came rushing across the street and stopped next to Clint.

Turning the man over Clint told the sheriff, "Apparently, one of the men you ran out of town decided to try and bushwhack me."

"Damn it!" Turner swore. "I hope the other three kept goin'."

Clint saw Gina standing at the door of the café, watching.

"How's your Pa?" he asked.

"He ain't complainin', but he's in pain. Didn't sleep all that good."

"Well," Clint said, "you might tell him he'll be getting a visitor later today."

"Oh? Who?"

Clint inclined his head toward the café.

"Oh, Gina," Thad said. "Maybe she'll cook. It's been a while since I had one of her home cooked meals."

"Why is that? I thought she and your Pa were friendly."

126

"She was friends with my Ma," Thad said. "Because of that, my Pa never felt it was decent for him to court Gina. But she keeps hopin'. I've got to get some men to remove this body."

"Aren't you going to tell me to get out of town?" Clint asked.

"No," the sheriff said. "I've decided the only way to get you to leave is to help you find out what you want to know."

"Your Pa was going to try to help me."

"I know, he told me," the young lawman said. "So now I'm gonna do the same."

"And how will you do that?"

"I don't know," Turner said, "but after I get this trash off the street, I'll give it some thought."

Chapter Thirty-One

J.B Patrick looked out the window of his hotel, down at Windham, South Dakota's main street. Then he turned and looked at McNee.

"How many men does it take to kill one?" he demanded.

"Sir—"

"How many has he killed, so far?"

"Well, Sir," McNee said, "four dead, and three run out of town."

"And how many do we have left?"

"I believe three," McNee said.

"Who?"

"The Morton brothers, Reese and Vance, and Charlie Bennett."

"Are they any good?"

"They're supposed to be."

Patrick looked out the window again.

"I'd like to be on the street when it happens," he said.

"Sir, you shouldn't leave the hotel room—"

"I know that!" Patrick snapped. "That's why I've been sitting in here for days. But I'm getting tired of waiting."

"It shouldn't be much longer," McNee said.

Patrick turned away from the window and pointed his finger at McNee.

"You'd better see to it!"

"How?"

"Go to see the Mortons and Bennett," Patrick said. "Tell them the price is now twenty-five hundred, but only if they get it done before the week is out."

"Yes, Sir."

"And let me know when you've seen them."

"Yes, Sir," McNee said, glumly. He was waiting impatiently for the moment they'd be able to leave Windham, South Dakota. He wanted to see the Deadwood Saloon where Wild Bill Hickok had been shot.

"Now get out!" J.B. Patrick bellowed.

"Yes, Sir."

McNee rushed from the room. A middle-aged man, he hated taking orders from someone in their twenties, but he didn't have much choice in the matter. The boy's father had left him everything, lock, stock and barrel, and that included McNee.

***

The Mortons and Charlie Bennett were still in The Bent Tree Saloon when McNee entered. The saloon was crowded, but he recognized the brothers.

"What the hell are you doin' here?" Reese Morton asked, as McNee approached their table.

"Looking for you," McNee said. "Is this Mr. Bennett?"

"That's right," Charlie Bennett said. "Who're you?"

"This is McNee," Reese told him. "He works for the man who's put up the bounty on Clint Adams."

"How is it you know who put up the money and nobody else does?" Bennett asked.

"My brother and I grew up with him," Reese said. "We told him not to send all those other guns, but he wouldn't listen."

"Well," McNee said, sitting, "now they're either dead or gone. Killing Adams is going to fall to you, and the price is now twenty-five hundred."

"After the way Adams has dealt with all the others," Vance Morton said, "it should be more than that."

"My brother's right," Reese said. "Since there's three of us, we want a thousand each."

"Three thousand dollars?" McNee asked, aghast.

"If your boss wants Adams dead bad enough, that price shouldn't be a bother to him."

"He wants the job done before the week is out," McNee told them.

"Get us our price, and it will be," Reese said.

"The price is acceptable," McNee told him. "Just get it done!"

"Don't you worry," Reese Morton said. "It'll get done."

McNee left the saloon without having a drink.

"Follow him," Reese told Vance. "I want to know where J.B. is."

"Right!" Vance said, and hurried out.

"Why do you wanna know where he is?" Charlie Bennett asked.

"Just in case we do the job and have to collect from him," Reese said.

"Ain't we supposed to go to the bank to collect the bounty?"

"Yeah," Reese said, "that's right, we're supposed to do that."

"You think this fella is gonna hold back the money?" Bennett asked.

"I wouldn't put it past him to try," Reese Morton said.

"Then why the hell are we workin' for the man?" Bennett asked.

"Don't worry," Reese said, "once the job's done I'll see to it that we get paid."

"We better," Bennett said. "We've already put a lot of time into this."

Chapter Thirty-Two

Clint was sitting in front of the hotel. If there were three gunmen left in town, he wanted it to be easy for them to find him. Instead, Sheriff Turner showed up. He pulled a chair over and sat next to Clint.

"What's on your mind?" Clint asked.

"I've been askin' around," Turner said.

"So have I," Clint pointed out.

"Well," Turner said, "maybe I was askin' questions you weren't."

"Meaning?"

"There's a man over at the Baily Hotel," Turner said. "He checked in several days ago—the day before you got here, as a matter of fact—and he hasn't been out of his room since."

"And you think that means what?"

"He might be the man who put the price on your head," Turner said.

"And he's waiting in his room for it to happen?" Clint asked. "Why doesn't he come out and watch?"

"Maybe he doesn't want you to recognize him."

"Well," Clint said, "maybe I should go over to the hotel and see this man."

"No," Turner said, "I'll do it. He doesn't have to open his door for you, but he does for me." Turner stood up. "I'll let you know what I find out."

"I'll wait right here, then," Clint said.

"There are three more gunmen in town," Turner told him. "Over at the Bent Tree. Stay away from there until I come back."

"You're not going to face them alone, are you?" Clint asked. "Gina would be mad as hell at me if anything happens to you."

"No," Turner said, "I'm just goin' to the hotel."

"Okay."

"Oh," Turner said, "by the way, Gina's gonna cook at my house tonight. Why don't you come?"

"Wouldn't your Pa rather be alone with her?"

"That's kind of the point," Turner said. "He doesn't."

"I'll be there."

Clint smiled and Sheriff Turner walked away.

***

Thad Turner went to the Bailey Hotel. The clerk let him look at the register book, which showed a Mr. Smith checked into room seven.

"It's our best room," the clerk told him.

"And have you seen him since he checked in?"

"No, Sir," the clerk said. "He hasn't come down that I know of."

"Not at all?" Turner asked. "What about his meals?"

"The other man brings them up to him."

"What other man?"

"He has a man workin' for him, Sheriff," the clerk said. "He's in room two, a small room."

"What's his name?"

The clerk looked at the register.

"Jones."

"Smith and Jones, huh?"

"That's right."

Turner stood there a moment, wondering if he should go up and see Smith or Jones? He decided to see the Smith, who was in the biggest room, who was being catered to by Jones.

"Okay, thanks," he said to the clerk, and went up the stairs.

He stopped in front of room two, just to listen at the door, but didn't hear anything inside. Then he walked up the hall to room seven and did the same thing.

***

When Vance Morton returned to the Bent Tree Saloon his brother Reese asked, "Where did he go?"

135

"The Bailey Hotel," Vance said.

"Sonofabitch!" Reese said. "That's where we're stayin'."

"You ain't seen him there?" Bennett asked.

"Hell, no."

"Maybe we should go and pay him a visit, then," Bennett said. "Make sure he's gonna meet our price."

"Charlie," Reese said, "I think that's a good idea."

The three men got up and left the saloon.

***

Sheriff Turner knocked on the door of room seven. When there was no answer he knocked again, harder. Hard enough to be heard down the hall. The door of room two opened, and McNee—who had registered as Jones—came running out.

"Can I help you?" he asked, hurrying up the hall.

Turner faced the man so he could see the badge.

"Oh, Sheriff . . ."

"Sheriff Turner, And you're Mr. Jones?"

"Uh, yes, that's right, Mr. Jones," McNee answered,

"Well, Mr. Jones," Turner said, "I'd like to speak to Mr. Smith."

"Actually," McNee said, "Mr. Smith speaks to the public through me."

"Is that right?" Turner asked. "Well, he's gonna have to speak to me himself. Open the door, please."

"Did you knock?"

"I did, but I assume you have a key."

"I do, but . . ."

"Open it, please."

McNee swallowed hard.

"Must I?"

"Yeah," Turner said, "you must."

McNee stepped to the door, knocked, said, "It's me, Sir," and then unlocked the door. "I have Sheriff Turner with me."

McNee swung the door open, and Turner stepped through. The man standing at the window turned and looked at him. He was young, but Turner could barely tell that. His face was scarred, he was leaning on a cane, and his body looked painfully twisted.

"What the hell do you want?" J.B. Patrick bellowed, in a surprisingly strong voice.

Chapter Thirty-Three

10 years ago . . .

Clint Adams looked at his friend Talbot Roper, lying in a hospital bed in Denver Memorial Hospital.

"Who was it?" he asked.

"Fella named Horace Patrick," Roper told him. "He didn't pull the trigger, but he sent those three men to ambush me."

"Well," Clint said, "the doctor says you're going to recover. Can't say the same for the three who came after you. You got them all."

"Now there's just Patrick," Roper said.

"You don't have to worry about him," Clint said. "Just tell me where to find him."

"I'm going to do just that," Roper said, "because by the time I get out of this bed, he'll be gone. But I don't want you to kill him."

"Why not?"

"Because I have all the proof I need to put him away for good," Roper said. "That's why he ambushed me."

Clint considered Talbot Roper the best private investigator in the country, so if he said he had all the proof he needed, that was good enough for him.

"Just bring him in to the police," Roper said. "I'll do the rest."

"Deal," Clint said. "Now tell me where to find him…"

***

Horace Patrick was a rich man, so he lived in a rich man's house in a rich part of town.

Clint followed Roper's directions, stood in front of the large, two-story Colonial, trying to figure the best way to get in. He finally decided on a direct approach. He went up the long walk to the front door and knocked. He was surprised when the door was opened by what looked to be a fourteen-year-old boy.

"I'm looking for Horace Patrick," he said.

"That's my Pa," the boy said. "I'm Jimmy."

"Well, Jimmy, where is your—"

"I told you not to open the door for anyone!" someone from inside the house roared.

A man came into view, fiftyish, short and wide, dressed well and fuming.

"Jimmy, damn it—who the hell are you?" the man demanded.

"My name's Clint Adams."

"I'm sorry, Pa—"

"Go to your room!" Patrick ordered. "I'll deal with you later."

"Yes, Pa." The boy ran up the long, broad flight of stairs.

"What the hell do you want?" Patrick demanded of Clint.

"You," Clint said. "You're coming with me to the police."

"Why would I do that?"

"Because if you don't," Clint said, "I'll kill you where you stand."

The man looked puzzled.

"Why the hell would you do that?" he demanded. "I don't even know you."

"But you know my friend, Talbot Roper," Clint said. "You had him ambushed, but it didn't work. He's still alive, he still has the evidence against you, and I'm taking you in. Now let's go."

The man glared at him, then looked defeated and said, "Let me get my coat."

He went to a door Clint assumed to be a closet, opened it, and came out not with a coat, but with a gun.

"You're not taking me—" he started, but Clint didn't let him finish.

To Clint's best recollection, he drew and fired, and as the bullet hit Patrick in the chest, he pulled the trigger of the gun he was holding. The house had been furnished with all the modern conveniences money could buy, and that included gas lamps on the walls. The bullet must have gone through the wall and punctured a gas pipe. There was an explosion, and suddenly the house was ablaze. The flames followed the gas all through the house, and while Clint wished he could have gotten upstairs to save the boy, it was impossible. He barely got out alive, himself.

Later the chief of the fire brigade told him that Horace Patrick's body was burned to a crisp. There was no one else in the house but the boy, Jimmy.

"I can't believe it," the chief said, "but he's alive, even though he's burned over about ninety per-cent of his body."

"Will he make it?" Clint asked.

"He's on his way to the hospital," the chief said, "but I've never seen anybody in that shape live."

Clint felt bad about the boy, but not about Horace Patrick. The man was a criminal who used his money and influence to build a criminal empire. Everything that had happened was a direct result of that lifestyle. Still, he wished he could have saved the boy.

When he left Denver, the boy was hanging on, but the doctors didn't have much hope. Over the years Clint wondered about him, but hadn't thought of him in a while . . .

Chapter Thirty-Four

"I have some questions for you, Mr. Smith," Sheriff Turner said.

"My man answers all my questions," the scarred man said. "I don't see people."

"Today you'll see me, Mr. Smith," Turner said, "or whatever your real name is."

"All right, ask your questions and be damned."

He walked, leaning painfully on the cane, to the bed and lowered himself into a seated position.

"Do you know a man named Clint Adams?" Turner asked.

"Of course I do," the man said. "I'm not ignorant. He's the Gunsmith."

"But do you know him beyond that?"

"As a matter of fact, I do," the man said. "He killed my father, and he's the reason I'm in this condition."

"So you put a price on his head?"

"Did I?" the man asked. "Can you prove that?"

"Probably not," Turner said, "but I think I've got it right. You put a price on his head, lured him here to this town, and sent a half dozen or more gunmen after him. You've got three left. I want you to call them off."

The scarred young man leaned on his cane and Turner thought his face might have been twisted in a smile.

"I think you should leave now, Sheriff," he said. "Mr. . . . Jones will show you out."

"I came to warn you," Turner said. "I'm gonna tell Adams you're here."

"Good," the man said. "It's been some time since I've seen him. Ten years, to be exact." He tapped the floor with his cane. "I think he should see what he did to me."

"Look," Turner said, "I don't know about your father, or why you think Adams is responsible—"

"I don't think it!" the man snapped. "I know it! I was there. I saw him shoot my father . . . and then the house exploded! Do you think I'd forget a thing like that, no matter how long I was in the hospital?"

"Sheriff—" McNee said.

"I know," Turner said. "I should leave. You're right, Mr. Smith. I can't prove it. But I don't think Clint Adams will wait for proof. Do you?"

Turner turned and left the room.

***

The Mortons and Charlie Bennett almost walked headlong into Sheriff Turner as he left the hotel. But they spotted him and his badge in time, to duck into the alley next to the hotel.

"What do you think he wanted?" Bennett asked, as they watched the sheriff walk away.

"I don't know," Reese Morton said. "But maybe we'll find out."

They went into the hotel lobby and saw McNee heading for the stairs.

"McNee!" Reese called.

The man stopped and turned.

"What are you doing here?" he asked.

When they reached him Reese said, "We came to see an old friend."

"Mr. Patrick won't see you," McNee said. "He doesn't see anyone."

"I'll bet he saw the sheriff," Reese said.

"You are not wearing a badge," McNee told him.

"We just wanted to check and see if our price was met," Bennett said.

"Yes," McNee said, "it has, you will receive a thousand dollars each the moment after you've killed the Gunsmith."

"Well," Reese said, "that's good to hear. But I'm, still kind of curious what the sheriff was doing here."

"That's none of your concern," McNee said. "Just get it done."

McNee turned and went up the stairs.

"He reminds me of a weasel," Bennett said.

"Yeah," Reese said, "I know what you mean."

"So whatta we gonna do, Reese?" Vance asked.

"Like the man said, little brother," Reese replied. "We're gonna get the job done."

Chapter Thirty-Five

Clint opened the door and allowed Sheriff Turner to enter his room.

"You find out anything?" he asked.

"I talked to two men named Smith and Jones."

"And?"

"And their real names aren't Smith and Jones."

"What are their real names?"

"I don't know."

"Did you ask?"

"I did," Turner said, "but they weren't talkin'. Mr. Smith seems to think you killed his father, and that you're responsible for his current condition."

"Condition?" Clint asked. "What condition?"

"Well, he's . . . scarred, and twisted," Turner said. "Needs a cane in order to walk."

"And he says I'm responsible?"

Turner added, "He sure does."

"Well, if he thinks that," Clint said, "maybe he's the one who put a price on my head."

"Maybe. He said he'd been in the hospital for a long time. Maybe he finally got out and decided to come after you."

"Well," Clint said, "maybe I should ask him."

"Maybe you should," Turner said, "but do me a favor, don't shoot 'im."

"As long as all he has in his hand is a cane," Clint said, "I won't."

"He's at the Bailey Hotel, room seven," Turner said. "When you're done, come and see me. Let me know how it went."

"I will," Clint said. "Maybe this whole thing can come to an end without any more bloodshed."

"I hope you're right."

Turner left the room, and Clint sat thinking about what the sheriff had said. He was trying to think who this man could be, and was coming up with only one person. But . . . it couldn't be him.

***

Clint entered the lobby of the Bailey Hotel, which looked slightly higher class than The Gregory. He bypassed the front desk and went right up the stairs. He knocked on the door of room seven and, after a moment, a voice called out, "Come in, I've been expecting you."

He opened the door with his left hand, keeping his right down by his gun. As he entered, a man standing at the window turned and looked at him. Clint saw what

Turner had meant about the man being scarred and twisted.

"Remember me, Mr. Adams?" the man asked, in a surprisingly strong voice.

"I'm afraid I don't, Mr. Smith," Clint said.

"Let me refresh your memory," the man said. "When we met, I told you my name was Jimmy."

And it all came flooding back. Horace Patrick, the fire in the Denver house, and the little boy who was burned so badly, he probably wouldn't survive.

"You thought I was dead, didn't you?" J.B. Patrick asked. "Believe me, there were many times I wanted to be. I was in the hospital for a long time—years. When I got out, I discovered what a rich man I was. And I started looking for you. Finding you wasn't hard, since you'd become more famous—or infamous—than you were ten years ago."

"Jimmy—" Clint started.

"I don't go by that name, anymore, Adams," Patrick said. "Now I'm J.B. Patrick."

"Mr. Patrick," Clint said, "what happened that night was a horrible accident."

"Was it?" He moved away from the window, leaning heavily on the cane. "Was it really? You shot and killed my father. I saw it. I was at the top of stairs. That's where I was when the fire started. Before I knew it, I was on fire."

"I wanted to try and get to you," Clint said, "but I couldn't. The heat was too intense."

"Sure," Patrick said, "you couldn't save me, or my father. That's what they told me in the hospital. For years I heard it was nobody's fault, just a terrible accident."

"Look—"

"No," Patrick said, "you look. There was nothing accidental about what happened that night. You killed my father, and started that fire—"

"Your father was a criminal—"

"That may be true," Patrick said, "but he was still my father. I decided even before I got out of the hospital that you were going to have to pay."

"So you put a price on my head." Put there not by no irate woman, or a vengeful man, but by a boy. That had never occurred to him.

"Why not?" Patrick asked. "After all, what's money for except to get you what you want." His voice became a growl. "And what I want is a dead Gunsmith!"

Chapter Thirty-Six

"You've got three guns left in town, Jimmy," Clint said.

"Don't call me that!"

"All right, *Mister* Patrick. After I've taken care of those three, what's next?"

"I've got plenty of money, Mr. Adams," Patrick said, "and my doctors tell me I have plenty of time."

"So you're going to keep this up?"

"Until you're dead."

"I could end it right here and now," Clint told him.

"By shooting me?" Patrick shook his head. "I've done my research, Adams. You don't shoot unarmed men. Now, everything is in my favor." The scarred face broke into an eerie looking smile. "You're as good as dead."

Clint stared at the scarred young man, then turned and left the room, and the hotel.

***

"He's right," Sheriff Turner told Clint, after hearing how the meeting had gone. "Unless you decide to put a bullet in him, everythin's in his favor."

"Where are these other three gunmen?" Clint asked.

"I don't know," Turner said. "Don't know where they are, or who they are."

"I guess I'll find that out, eventually," Clint said.

"I do have one more play," Turner said.

"What's that?"

"I can run him out of town. Maybe if he's not here to see it, he'll call it off."

"I doubt that," Clint said. "He wants me dead whether he can see it or not."

"Is he right?" Turner asked. "Did you kill his father?"

"I did," Clint said. "He was a criminal I was trying to take in, and he pulled a gun on me. I shot him, but his shot went wild and struck a gas pipe. It set the house on fire."

"And this fella was burned," Turner finished. "That doesn't sound like your fault, Adams."

"I never thought it was," Clint said. "I mean, I felt bad about what happened to the boy, but I never felt any guilt or remorse."

"Maybe you should."

"What?"

"Maybe that's what he wants."

"You think he'll call it off if I show remorse and apologize?"

"No, you're right," Turner said. "If somebody killed my father, I'd want more than an apology."

"How is your father, by the way?"

"He's goin' crazy sittin' at home," Turner said. "By the way, you're still comin' tonight, right? Gina's cookin'."

"I'll be there."

"Good. Maybe my Pa will have some advice for you. Come by around eight. Gina has to finish up at the café."

"I'll see you at eight," Clint said, "providing I'm not gunned down in the street between now and then."

Clint started for the door but stopped when Turner said, "One more thing."

"What's that?"

"The fella who works for Smith, or Patrick, whatever his name is. The one callin' himself Jones. Did you see him?"

"No, I didn't."

"I don't know if he'll be somebody you know from ten years ago, but maybe you can get him to talk some sense into Patrick."

"For a young fella," Clint said, "you have some good ideas. I'll try that."

Clint left and headed back to the Bailey Hotel.

***

Clint stopped at the front desk of the Bailey.

"What room is Mr. Jones in?" he asked.

"Room two, Sir."

"Thanks."

He went up the stairs and knocked on the door of room two. The man who answered was small, in his fifties, and reminded Clint of a weasel. He had never seen him before.

"Mr. Jones?"

"That's right."

"I'm Clint Adams."

"I know," the man said. "Mr. Patrick told me you saw him earlier today. Come in."

Clint entered. The room was half the size of J.B. Patrick's.

"Your name's not Jones," he said.

"No, it's not," the man said. "It's McNee."

"Did you work for Jimmy's father, Mr. McNee?"

"I did," McNee said, "but I wasn't around . . . that day."

"I guess you were lucky."

"I was left to young Mr. Patrick in his father's will," McNee said, "so that depends on how you define lucky."

"Mr. McNee," Clint said, "what happened ten years ago wasn't my fault."

"Oh, I know that, Mr. Adams."

"Have you ever tried to convince Jimmy of that?"

"I have," McNee said, "but he's very stubborn."

"You can't convince him to call this off?" Clint asked.

"Believe me, Mr. Adams, I wish I could. He's very committed."

"So he doesn't listen to you?"

"Not at all," McNee said. "I'm simply his public face. In his condition, he prefers not to be seen."

"Just how rich is he, McNee?"

"Rich enough to buy my self-respect," McNee said.

"How long was he in the hospital?"

"Years," McNee said. "His recovery was painstakingly slow. They virtually had to try to rebuild his body, and you saw the result."

"But what about his mind?" Clint asked.

"I—I can't discuss something like that," McNee said. "I've been employed by the Patrick family for many, many years."

"I appreciate that you're loyal, Mr. McNee, but your boss is not going to get away with this."

"Mr. Adams," McNee said, "you have to do what you have to do, and I have to do what I have to do."

"I suppose you're right," Clint said.

"I wish I could help you," McNee said, "but right now I have to go and see to Mr. Patrick."

"Do you ever call him Jimmy?" Clint asked.

"Never," McNee said, looking horrified.

Chapter Thirty-Seven

The sheriff had given Clint directions to his small house at the far edge of town. When he knocked, the door was opened by Gina, the waitress from the café. Only she looked different. She was wearing a dress that clung to her, and her hair was down. Clint wondered what was wrong with Liam Turner if he wasn't interested.

"Hello, Mr. Adams," she said.

"It's Clint, Gina" he said. "Just Clint."

"Come on in," she said. "I have to get back to the kitchen, but Liam is sittin' on the sofa. The Sheriff's not here, yet, but he should be soon."

He followed her as she led him to where Liam was sitting, and then continued on into the kitchen.

"Smells good in here," he said to Deputy Turner.

"I guess so." Turner had a sour look on his face.

"Ribs still hurt?"

"Like hell."

Clint saw that the man was holding an empty glass.

"Want me to fill that for you?"

"Hey, yeah, thanks," Turner said, holding the empty glass out. "There's a bottle over there. Pour a drink for yourself, too."

"Thanks."

Clint walked over to a sideboard by a window where there were several bottles of liquor and glasses. He poured two fingers of whiskey into two glasses, carried one back to Liam Turner.

"Thanks," Turner said. "I'm goin' crazy just sittin' here. I gotta get back to work." He sipped his drink. "Thad told me what's been goin' on. So you found out some cripple put the price on your head?"

"I guess you could call him that," Clint said. "I think he's a kid who's gone kind of crazy. Though I can't blame him for that."

"A kid?"

"He's about your son's age."

"Not a kid, then," Turner said.

At that moment the front door opened, and Sheriff Turner walked in.

"Smells good," he said. "And I'll have a drink." He got himself a whiskey and sat next to his father on the sofa.

"How are you, Pa?"

"I was just tellin' Adams, here, that I'm goin' crazy. And we were talkin' about the cripple."

"You talk to the other one?" Sheriff Turner asked.

"Jones?"

"His real name's McNee," Clint said, "and there's nothing he can do. He says Jimmy Patrick is committed to having me killed."

"Well, that settles it, then," the sheriff said. "Tomorrow I'll kick him and this McNee out of town. They'll have to hear about your death some other way."

"That's very encouraging," Clint said.

Gina came out of the kitchen and asked, "Are you boys hungry?"

Chapter Thirty-Eight

The four of them ate together at the kitchen table. Clint noticed that the interaction between Gina and Liam was very strained. She was, however, motherly in her treatment of Thad, and he seemed receptive, even though she wasn't quite old enough to be his mother. Clint figured Gina was about ten years younger than Liam, in her mid-forties.

When Liam finished his plate of chicken and vegetables he said, "Thanks, Gina," and limped back to the sofa.

"This was really great, Gina," the young sheriff said.

"Yes, it was delicious," Clint said.

"I'll just clear the dishes and clean the kitchen before I leave," Gina told Thad. Then she looked at Clint. "Mr. Adams, when I'm done will you walk me home?"

"It would be my pleasure," Clint said.

Clint and Thad left the kitchen. Liam wasn't on the sofa.

"Pa probably went to his room," Thad said.

"He's really not interested in Gina, is he? I mean, as a woman."

"No," Thad said, "it's been years, but he's still in love with my mother."

"I guess I can understand that."

"I feel sorry for Gina," Thad said. "She's a great gal."

"She seems to be."

Gina came out of the kitchen and said, "It's all clean." She went to Thad and kissed his cheek. "Take care of that crusty old man."

"I will," he said.

"Ready?" she asked Clint.

"Let's go," he said.

They left the house and began walking. It had already gotten dark.

"I don't live far," she said.

"That's okay," he said. "A walk in the night air would be nice . . . relaxing."

She folded her arms as they walked side-by-side.

"I think I'm ready to give up," she said.

"Give up? On what?"

"Not what," she said. "Who. Liam."

"Oh."

"He's clearly not interested in me as anything but a waitress."

"It's hard to compete with a man's dead wife," Clint said.

"Yes, it is," she said. "And I'm tired of trying. This is mine."

They stopped in front of a house that was larger than the sheriff's.

"I'm impressed," he said.

"Don't be," she said. "This was left to me by my parents when they died, over twenty years ago."

They walked to the front door, and he waited while she unlocked it.

"Would you mind coming in for a little while?" she asked. "I think I need the company."

"Sure."

They entered the house, and she made her way in the dark to a lamp, which she lit. In the yellow glow Clint saw a comfortably furnished interior, with an overstuffed sofa and two matching chairs. There was a dining area with a long, wooden table. The place seemed spotlessly clean.

"I'd like a glass of wine," she said. "How about you?"

"Why not?"

She poured two glasses of red wine and handed him one, then stretched. The movement pulled the fabric of her dress even tighter to her body, which was fulsome.

"My shoulders hurt," she said. "Think you could rub them for me?"

"I don't know how good I'll be at it," he said, putting the glass of wine down, "but I'll give it a try."

He put his hands on her shoulders and started to rub. She sighed and he could feel her muscles relaxing.

"How's that?" he asked.

"It's good," she said, "but it might be better this way."

She reached behind her, undid her dress and slid it down off her shoulders, leaving them bare. Her skin was soft and velvety and very warm. He continued to massage her shoulders, and she let her head fall back, then turned into him and raised her chin for a kiss.

"Gina—"

"I told you, Clint," she said, "I'm through waiting for a man who's not interested in me." She slid her hand down the front of his pants and squeezed his already hard cock. "You feel interested."

He kissed her . . .

Chapter Thirty-Nine

Gina took Clint's hands and led him into her bedroom. She pulled the quilt and top sheet down, discarded her dress and crawled into her large, four-poster bed. He watched as the muscles in her butt and thighs bunched and relaxed. Apparently, waiting tables kept her in fine condition, even in her mid-forties.

He undressed, set his gun aside, within easy reach, and joined her on the bed. She gathered him into her arms, and he was impressed by the strength of her. She was a woman both soft and strong.

He kissed the flesh of her neck and shoulders while her hands were busy on him. Her breasts were large, slightly pendulous because of her age, but still firm enough. The nipples were dark and extended so that they were easy and pleasing to nibble on.

She sighed and cupped his head as he worked on her breasts with his mouth, then moved further down, over her belly to between her thighs, where she was soaking wet.

"Jesus," she said, as he touched her with his tongue, "no one's ever done that before—ohhh, yes, keep doing that . . ."

He did, lapping up her juices as they flowed and then holding her down with his elbows on her thighs, his mouth still working as her body trembled with pleasure and exploded in release . . .

***

"Well," she said breathlessly, moments later, this makes me wonder what I've been waiting for all this time." She rolled onto her side to look at him. "Is this what people are doing these days?"

"I don't know what people are doing these days," he said, "but it's what I do."

"And you do it very well, Sir."

"Thank you."

She reached down and touched his cock, which was still very hard.

"There are things I've never done that I'd like to do," she said. "Do you mind?"

"I'll try to bear it," he said.

She giggled, then slid down so that she could kiss his thighs and rub his hard penis against her cheeks.

"God," she said, "you're such a beautiful man . . ."

She took the bulging head of his cock into her mouth gingerly, wetting it, sucking it lightly, then became bolder and took more. She seemed to surprise and delight herself with how much of him she could take. She began to suck him avidly, her head bobbing up and down. Finally, she could wait no longer to mount him and take him inside her hot, wet depths.

She began to ride him, slowly at first, but then her tempo increased as she closed her eyes, bit her lips and chased her climax . . .

***

"Oh God," she said, putting her hands over her face. "Oh Jesus, what am I gonna do when you leave town?"

"What do you mean?"

"I've had sex with men before, Clint, but not for many years. I have pretty much been living a sexless life. But after this . . ." She reached over and grabbed his cock. "What am I gonna do without this?"

She sounded desperate. It made him think back to wondering if it was a woman who had put the price on his head, a woman he had perhaps left behind, mired in desperation. Ultimately, that had not been the case, but he didn't like how intensely Gina seemed to have fixated on him.

"Gina—" he started, but she stopped him.

"Oh, relax," she said. "I'm a grown woman and I know this doesn't mean anything. I'm just wondering where else I'll be able to get this." She squeezed his cock again, and it started to react.

"Oh, my," she said, "again?"

"Well," he said, "you *are* giving it a lot of attention."

"Then," she said, lying on her back and spreading her legs wide, "how about hopping on and really giving me something to remember you by?"

"If you insist," he said.

He mounted her and drove his cock into her, grabbed her legs by the ankles, held them apart and began to fuck her brutally. She had ridden him with her eyes closed, her head back, concerned only with her own release, so he decided to do exactly the same thing.

She grabbed hold of the sheets on either side of her as he continued to slam into her, giving her exactly what she wanted even though he was only thinking of himself.

Finally, when he exploded into her, she let out a loud roar that seemed to startle her, but she wrapped her thighs around his waist as he released his hold on her ankles, and cried out as he continued to empty out into her . . .

Chapter Forty

Reese Morton woke that morning and decided this was the day. He looked over at his brother in the other bed, then at each of their whores. His was a long and lean brunette who was lying on her tummy, snoring gently. Vance's girl was blonde, too bosomy to lie on her belly, he watched her big tits move with her breathing.

"Hey!" he snapped.

Nobody woke up.

He grabbed his pillow and threw it at the other bed. The blonde sat right up as it struck her, but his brother continued to sleep.

"What?" she said, looking around.

"Switch!" he snapped and slapped the brunette on the ass. She stirred. "Change partners."

The blonde swung her legs around, putting her feet on the floor, and stood up. She came to Reese's bed and shook the brunette.

"They wanna switch," she said. "Come on, Lily."

"Yeah, yeah, okay," the brunette said. She went to Vance's bed, was happy to see he was still asleep, so she stretched out next to him on her stomach and dropped off again. Neither she nor Vance was aware of the noise Reese and the blonde were making in the other bed . . .

***

Reese paid the two girls, then he and his brother left the room, and the whorehouse.

"I didn't get to switch," Vance complained.

"That's what you get for sleepin' so soundly," Reese said.

"Are we gettin' breakfast?"

"We get breakfast," Reese said, "and then we get the Gunsmith."

"What about Charlie?"

"We'll go and wake him up now," Reese said.

"You think he'll be ready?"

"He better be," Reese said. "He's the one says what a fast gun he is."

"What about Jimmy?" Vance asked.

Reese and Vance had known Jimmy when they were all boys in Denver, but they had lost contact after the fire. It was only recently that Jimmy had found them—well, McNee did—and brought them to Windham to kill the Gunsmith.

"This is gonna make us big men, Vance," Reese told his brother. "Big men!"

"And rich men."

"That, too."

"How are we gonna do it?" Vance asked.

"Relax," Reese told him, "I got a plan . . ."

***

Clint woke with Gina lying on his left shoulder, which was fine because it left his right hand free. But the light coming in through the window told him it was time to get moving. He had a feeling today was going to be the day everything came to a head. Sheriff Turner planned to order J.B. Patrick and McNee out of town, and that might force Patrick to put his last three gunmen to work. But if and when Clint was able to take care of them, that still left a rich man out there who was willing to spend all his money to murder the Gunsmith. It was bad enough Clint had to deal with his reputation on a daily basis. Having to deal with a rich man's vengeance would make each day that much harder to get through.

As he slid his arm from beneath Gina, she moaned and stirred.

"Sorry," he said.

She looked at him, then at the window, then came fully awake.

"That's okay," she said. "I have to get to the café for breakfast."

They both got out of bed and took turns washing and dressing.

"Wow," she said, stretching, pressing her hands to her lower back, "what a night."

"I agree."

"What are you gonna do today?" she asked.

"Oh, I just thought I'd try to stay alive," he told her.

"Isn't Thad gonna take care of those men at the hotel?" she asked.

"He's going to try," Clint said, "but even if he does get them to leave town, that won't be the end of it."

"So when will it end?"

He shrugged.

"Either when the rich man runs out of money," he said, "or I'm dead, whichever comes first."

She stared at him a long moment, then said, "That's not funny."

"Believe it or not," he told her, "I wasn't trying to be funny."

Chapter Forty-One

As Thad Turner came into the living room, he saw his father strapping on his gun.

"What do you think you're doin'?" he asked.

"I'm goin' with you," he said. "I ain't lettin' you face that crazy cripple without no backup."

"He's a cripple, Pa," Turner said. "I don't need no backup."

"I don't care what you say," Liam said, "I'm your deputy and I'm goin' with ya."

"Yeah, okay," Thad said, watching his father move painfully toward the door.

***

Clint decided to have breakfast at Gina's café, and she gave him a feast.

"Just leave it to me," she had told him. She brought out flapjacks, bacon-and-eggs and biscuits.

"A reward for a job well done," she said, as she laid the plates down.

"Thank you, Ma'am."

Clint finished most of the food and washed it down with a pot of coffee. When he stood up to leave, Gina came rushing over.

"What if you just left town?" she asked.

"That price on my head would always follow me around," he told her. "It has to all end here, one way or another."

She put her hand on his arm.

"Try not to let anything happen to you, or to them."

"I'll try my damnedest," he promised, and left.

***

Sheriff Thad Turner and Deputy Liam Turner entered the lobby of The Bailey Hotel.

"What if you stay down here in the lobby, just in case?" Thad suggested.

"Not a chance," Liam said. "Just quiet down, son, and lead the way."

They went up the stairs, passed room two and walked directly to room seven. The first time Sheriff Turner knocked, there was no answer.

"Patrick!" he shouted, banging again. "It's the Sheriff. Come on, I know you're in there."

From down the hall the door to room two opened and McNee came rushing out.

"Gentlemen, gentlemen—" he started, but it was Liam who cut him off.

"Never mind the crap," he snapped. "Get your boss to open the door!"

"I—I have a key," McNee said.

"Then open it," Sheriff Turner told him.

"Sheriff," McNee said, "just what is it you have in mind?"

"You and your boss are leavin' town," Sheriff Turner said. "Now!"

"I—but—"

The sheriff grabbed the key from McNee's hand and unlocked the door. As the three men entered, they saw J.B. Patrick, seated on the end of the bed, leaning on his cane.

"Mr. Patrick?" McNee said. "Sir?"

"What's wrong with 'im?" Sheriff Turner asked.

"Nothin'!" Liam snapped. "He's fakin'. Watch."

The deputy walked to the seated man, put his hand on his shoulder, then pulled it away.

"Pa?" Sheriff Turner said.

The deputy turned and looked at his son.

"I think he's dead."

"What?" the sheriff said.

Liam stepped aside as McNee approached and examined the man.

174

"Yes," McNee said, "he's quite dead." He looked at the two lawmen. "It was probably his heart."

"Then it's over," Sheriff Turner said.

"I'm afraid not," McNee said.

"What's that?" Liam demanded. "Why not?"

"Well, for one thing, there are still three gunmen out there," McNee said. "And the money is still out there."

"Call it back," Turner said.

"I don't have the authority."

"So even with him dead, there's a reward for the Gunsmith?" the sheriff asked.

"I'm afraid so," McNee said. "The bank has orders to pay it out."

"We'll see about that," the sheriff said. "Meanwhile, you go pack your bags."

"Me?"

"That's right," the lawman said. "You're leavin' town, with your boss' body."

The sheriff started for the door.

"Where you goin'?" the deputy asked.

"You stay here and make sure he packs," Turner said and left.

Chapter Forty-Two

Sheriff Turner saw Clint Adams coming out of Gina's café.

"What's the hurry?" Clint asked as the young sheriff rushed up to him.

"It's that cripple fella, Patrick."

"What about him?"

"He's dead."

"Dead?" Clint asked. "What happened?"

"Don't know," Turner said. "We went into his room, and he was sitting up on the edge of the bed, leaning on his cane, and he was just . . . dead. I'm gonna have the doc take a look at 'im."

"What about McNee?"

"I told him he's gotta get out of town and take the body with 'im."

"What about the price on my head?"

"McNee says he can't pull it."

"That's crazy."

"He says the money's in the bank, and it'll be paid when the deed is done."

"There's got to be something you can do," Clint said. "Talk to the bank manager."

"I'll do that, and we'll see what happens. Meanwhile, I'm goin' over to Doc's."

"I'll come with you."

As they walked Turner said, "Those green gunmen are still in town. Maybe if we find 'em and tell 'em Patrick's dead, they'll pull out."

"Not if they know they can still get paid at the bank."

"Yeah, right."

At the doctor's office Clint waited outside while Turner went in and spoke with the sawbones.

"He's gonna go over and take a look at the body," Turner said, when he came out.

"Where's your Pa?" Clint asked.

"He's at the hotel, makin' sure McNee is packin' to leave."

"I wonder where those three guns are," Clint said. "It's too early for the saloons."

"Maybe they're havin' breakfast somewhere," Turner said, "a man don't like to kill or be killed on an empty stomach."

"I don't think it's a good idea to wait until they find me," Clint said. "I'm thinking I ought to find them and push them."

"You'll have to kill 'em."

"Unless I can talk them out of it."

"I guess that would depend on what the price on your head is now."

"You think Patrick increased it?"

"After what happened with all the other gunnies, that's what I'd do."

"Well then," Clint said, "I better start looking."

"I can come along and back you."

"You're the law," Clint said. "If you're there, nothing will happen. I need this to be finished. Why don't you walk back to the hotel with the doctor? Depending on what he says Patrick died of, you can get McNee going with the body."

"He'll need a buckboard," Turner said. "I can get 'im one."

"I'll come over to the Bailey Hotel if anything happens," Clint said.

"All right," Turner said. "There are a few cafés at the south end of town. You might check there."

"Right."

The doctor, a tall man in his forties, came out of his office, carrying his black bag.

"Ready, Doc?" Turner asked.

"I'm ready, Sheriff."

Clint and the other two men went their separate ways.

***

The Morton brothers woke Charlie Bennett at the Bailey and they had breakfast in the dining room. They didn't see the two lawmen enter the hotel and didn't see Sheriff Turner leave.

"That's your plan?" Bennett asked. "I face Adams."

"You keep sayin' how fast you are," Reese said. "We'll back your play. Beatin' the Gunsmith will make you a big man."

"You're right about that," Bennett said, rubbing his jaw.

"Come on, Charlie," Vance said. "You can beat 'im."

"Yeah," Bennett said, "yeah, I can."

Reese took his napkin out of his shirt, dropped it on the table and said, "Let's go find 'im."

They left the dining room and went out the front door. As they did, they saw two men coming toward them, and one was the sheriff.

"Whatta we do?" Vance asked.

"Charlie," Reese said, "he's all yours."

***

As Sheriff Turner and the doctor approached the hotel, three men came out the front door. Turner recognized them as the last of the three gunmen who were in town. He and the doctor stopped walking.

"I was lookin' for you three gents," Turner lied. "Time for you to leave town."

"And why would that be, Sheriff?" Reese asked.

"Your boss is dead."

"What?"

"Yeah," Turner said, "he died some time durin' the night."

"Of what?" Reese asked.

"This is the doctor," Turner said. "He's gonna find out. So you see, there's no more pay day."

"Naw, naw," Reese said, "the money's in the bank. All we gotta do is kill Adams and go collect it."

"I can't let you boys do that," Turner said.

"How you gonna stop us, Sheriff?" Reese asked. He and Vance were standing on either side of Charlie Bennett.

"The hard way, if you make me," Turner said. "Doc, move aside."

The doctor did as he was told.

"Charlie . . ." Reese said.

"He's wearin' a badge, Reese."

"A thousand dollars each, Charlie," Reese reminded him.

"Right."

Charlie Bennett drew his gun and fired . . .

***

Clint wasn't too far away to hear the first shot, and one right after it. He started running toward the Bailey Hotel. As he approached, he saw the doctor leaning over somebody lying on the ground.

"Damnit," he swore, as he got closer and saw that it was the sheriff.

"How is he?" Clint asked.

The doctor looked up.

"He's alive, but I've got to get that bullet out."

"Who did it?"

"Three men who came out of the hotel," the doctor said. "The Sheriff told them to get out of town. One of them gunned him down, beat him to the draw clean. Thad got one shot off into the ground."

"Where'd they go?" Clint asked.

"I don't know," the doctor said, "but before you go looking for them, you've got to help me carry the sheriff inside. I need to get him into a bed."

"Okay," Clint said, "and put him in room seven."

Chapter Forty-Three

"What the hell happened?" Liam Turner shouted as they came down the hall carrying his son.

"One of those gunnies shot him," Clint said.

"They ambushed him?"

"No," the doctor said, "he outdrew him clean."

Liam looked at Clint.

"He had to be fast to do that."

"Get that body off the bed!" the doctor snapped.

"Now wait a minute—" McNee complained.

"Shut up!" Liam said. He knocked J.B. Patrick's twisted body to the floor, then helped Clint and the doctor lay Thad on the bed.

"Is he gonna be okay, Doc?" Liam asked.

"That depends," the doctor said. "The bullet's in his chest, but it hopefully missed his heart. I'll know more when I start digging for it."

McNee said, "What about Mister Patrick?"

"He's already dead. I'll look at his body after I'm finished here."

"You better stay here, Liam," Clint said to the deputy.

"Where are you goin'?"

"After those guns," Clint said. "They shot a lawman."

"That means I oughtta go after 'em," Deputy Turner said.

"You stay here and hope your boy survives," Clint said. "I'll take care of those three."

"You want a badge?" Liam asked. "With Thad down, I'm authorized to deputize you."

"I don't need a badge for what I've got to do," Clint told him.

"You can bring 'em in," Liam said, "or kill 'em, I don't care which."

"I'll let them call the play," Clint said, "but I'll go either way. First, I'm going to stop at the bank, see if I can get that money pulled."

"Good luck," Liam said. "You tell that bank manager Grimes if he don't do it, he'll have to deal with me."

"I'll tell him."

Clint left the hotel and headed for the bank.

***

"Mr. Adams," Grimes said, "I wish I could help—"

"The man who put up the bounty is dead, Mr. Grimes," Clint said, "and now the sheriff has been shot.

And when I get through there won't be anyone to collect the bounty."

"Mr. Adams," Grimes said, "I'm just the bank manager. I'll have to talk to the board of directors."

"You do that," Clint said. "But the deputy wanted me to tell you, if you don't get this done, you'll have to deal with him."

Grimes swallowed hard and blinked behind his glasses.

"And if the sheriff dies . . ."

"I-I understand, Mr. Adams," Grimes said. "I'll do my best."

"I'll check back in with you," Clint said, and left.

***

The streets were deserted as Clint headed back to the hotel. There had already been a shooting, and people felt it wasn't over yet.

Clint decided to just walk down the center of the main street and call the men out.

"I don't know your names," he shouted, "but I'm calling out to the men who shot Sheriff Turner. If you want the bounty that's on my head, come and get it."

He kept walking, keeping a sharp eye out.

A Price on a Gunsmith's Head

***

The Mortons and Charlie Bennett were in an alley, keeping an eye on the hotel. They had seen Clint Adams come out, but they weren't ready yet. Now they saw him walking down the street, alone and with no backup.

"There he is," Reese said, "ripe for the pickin'."

"Why don't we just gun 'im down now?" Vance said, aiming his rifle. "He'll never know what hit 'im."

"And if we miss?" Reese said. "Or worse, wound him, it'd be like woundin' a bear. Naw, we gotta give Charlie his chance. Right, Charlie?"

"Right," Bennett said. He touched his gun, made sure it was loose in the holster.

"You step on out there and get it done," Reese said. "We got you covered."

Bennett nodded, and stepped out of the alley.

***

Clint saw the lone man coming out of the alley and move into the street.

"You the man who shot the sheriff?" he asked.

"That's right."

"What's your name?"

185

"Charlie Bennett."

"Never heard of you."

"Folks will," Bennett said, "after I kill you."

"You think that's likely?"

"I do."

"Where are your partners?" Clint asked.

"They ain't around," the man said. "It's just me."

"You're a little older than they are," Clint said. "You should be smarter."

"You know," Bennett said, "for a living legend, you sure do talk too much."

"I'm just trying to figure out what I can say to get you to walk away."

"Ha!" Bennett said. "Nothing!"

"Well," Clint said, "I tried."

Bennett drew his gun. Clint could see how he had outdrawn Thad Turner. There was no tell, and he was fast. Almost fast enough.

Clint drew and shot Bennett in the chest. The man's hand opened, his gun fell to the ground, and then he followed, falling onto his face. Clint looked around quickly for the other two, but they weren't around. They might've been in the alley Bennett stepped out of, but he doubted they were there now.

He walked to Bennett and checked the body. He was dead. He ejected his spent shell, reloaded and holstered his gun.

One down, two to go.

Chapter Forty-Four

Just to be sure, Clint checked the alley. There were enough boot prints in the dirt to indicate they had been there, but now they were gone. Had they run off? Or just withdrew to regroup?

Now that they knew their fast gun was dead, as well as the money man, what would their next move be?

And then it hit him.

***

"This was the plan all along?" Vance asked, as they approached the bank with their horses.

"Yeah," Reese said, "while Charlie keeps Adams busy, we rob the bank. It don't matter if J.B.'s alive or dead, we're after more than just the price on the Gunsmith's head."

"You're brilliant, Reese," Vance said.

"I know, little brother," Reese said. "That's why I make all the plans."

They tied off their mounts, entered the bank and both stuck their guns in the face of Grimes, the young bank manager.

"Put it all in bags," Reese told him.

"But—but—"

"You heard 'im," Vance said. "Empty the vault, or you're a dead man."

Sweating profusely, Grimes obeyed.

"All right," Reese said, when they had the bag of money, "don't stick your head out that door, or I'll shoot it off."

"Y-yessir!"

Reese and Vance backed their way to the door, then turned, opened it and rushed out. They both stopped short when they saw Clint Adams standing in the street.

***

Clint hoped he was guessing right, but what other move could they make if they wanted money? He stopped when he got to the bank and saw the two horses tied out front. He couldn't see inside, but it certainly looked like he had guessed right. Just then the front door of the bank opened, and two men came rushing out. One of them carried a bag of money. They both stopped short when they saw him there.

"I made a good guess," he told them. "Drop the bag, and your guns."

"Charlie?" Reese said.

"He made a good try," Clint said, "but he's dead."

"Damn!" Vance swore. "Reese—"

"Shut up," Reese said. "We ain't givin' up now."

"It's all over, boys," Clint said. "Bennett's dead, Patrick's dead and you're going to join them if you don't do what I tell you."

"We can't do that," Reese said. "We come too far."

"Then you've got one choice left."

Reese went for his gun, totally surprising his brother, who then grabbed for his in a panic.

Clint drew smoothly and shot both men before they could clear leather. The bag of money hit the ground, and then the Morton brothers toppled over. Suddenly, people started coming out onto the street. Grimes looked out the front window of the bank, then came running out, shouting, "Omigod, omigod!" and grabbed the bag of money.

"Take the money back inside, Grimes," Clint said. "I don't think anybody else is going to be trying to collect on my head today."

"I'm gonna do my best, Mr. Adams," Grimes said. "I swear, my best to get that bounty off your head. Thank you, thank you."

He ran back into the bank.

Clint turned and headed for the hotel.

Chapter Forty-Five

By the time Clint got to The Bailey Hotel, the doctor had the bullet out of Sheriff Turner's chest. Deputy Turner turned and looked at him as he entered the room.

"What was all the shootin'?" Turner asked.

"It's over," Clint said, and explained what had happened with Bennett and the brothers.

"Looks like you took care of 'em all," the deputy said.

"How is he?" Clint asked, nodding toward the bed.

"I got the bullet," the doctor said. "Now the rest is up to him."

"And what do I do now?" McNee asked.

The doctor walked over to examine J.B. Patrick's body.

"It looks to me like his heart just gave out," he said. "This man seems to have been through a lot."

"I'll get some men to carry him down," Deputy Turner said to McNee, "and I'll get you a buckboard. You're leavin' town."

"There's also three bodies in the street," Clint told Turner.

"I'll handle it," he said. "You've done enough."

"I'll come down with you."

"I'm going to stay with my patient for a while," the doctor said "He's gonna need constant care."

Clint thought about Gina and said, "I think I know just the person."

Clint and the deputy left the room, taking McNee with them as far as his room, to collect his bags.

***

By late that afternoon, McNee had driven out of town with J.B. Patrick's body, and the three gunmen had been collected from the street and taken to the undertaker's office.

While Deputy Turner took care of all that, Clint went and told Gina what happened. Just as he figured, she rushed from the café to the hotel to be at Thad Turner's side.

When Clint got to the sheriff's office, Turner was seated behind the desk, looking pained.

"Ribs?" Clint asked.

"Hurts like a sonofabitch," Turner said.

"I guess maybe they are cracked," Clint said. "Not much you can do about that."

"I'll just keep workin'," Turner said, "and try to keep my mind off the pain." He stood up. "I was about to go back to the hotel to check on Thad."

"Gina's there," Clint said. "Between her and the doctor, he'll have great care."

"I'm gonna have to do a lot of talkin' to him when he gets on his feet," Liam Turner said. "I don't think he thought anybody would ever outdraw him."

"He said you were faster than him."

"At one time, maybe," Liam said. "But you, of all people, know we're always gonna meet somebody faster."

Clint thought about how fast Charlie Bennett was and said, "It's going to happen to all of us, eventually."

"I'm gonna go over and see my boy, now," Liam said. "What are your plans?"

"I'll be leaving town in the morning," Clint said.

"Then let's have supper later," Liam said. "The town owes you that, at least."

Clint grinned and said, "Agreed."

They left the office together, and while the deputy headed for The Bailey Hotel to check on his son, Clint headed for his hotel to just take a couple of hours of well-deserved rest. He would meet up with the deputy later for supper and get a report on the sheriff's condition.

He hoped the young bank manager, Grimes', best would be good enough to convince the bank board to remove the bounty money from their deposits, but he didn't know if he would even find that out before he left town.

***

Clint met up with Deputy Turner later that evening, and while Gina was not waiting tables they still went to the café for their meal.

"How's Thad doing?" Clint asked.

"He ain't no worse," Turner said. "Doc says if he makes it through the night, he'll probably be all right. Gina's gonna stay with him."

"She's a great lady," Clint said.

"Yeah, I guess she is."

"She thinks a lot of the two of you."

"I know what she wants," Liam said, "I just can't give it to her."

"I get it," Clint said. "Luckily, she still wants to help."

They both ordered steak dinners and had a beer while they waited.

"I talked with Grimes today," Turner said.

"Is he still waiting to hear from his board?" Clint asked.

"I convinced him to do away with that deposit," Turner said.

"What's he going to do with that money?"

"We'll put it toward buryin' all those would-be gunnies you took care of," Turner said. "Then use the rest of it for town improvements."

"So it's over," Clint said.

"You won't have to keep lookin' over your shoulder, anymore."

"I wish that was true," Clint said, "but at least I don't have to worry about having a price on my head. Makes me wonder how outlaws can live that way."

"Everybody's got their own way of life," Turner said, as the waiter brought their meals. "Right now, all we got to worry about are these steaks."

"Agreed!" Clint said.

Chapter Forty-Six

The next morning, after breakfast, Clint collected the Tobiano from the livery stable, happy that they were both going to stretch their legs. He walked the horse over to The Bailey Hotel, checked on Thad Turner with Gina, who said he had made it through the night all right.

"Doc says he should be all right," she said. "Are you leaving now?"

"Yes," Clint said. "It's time for me to get back to my life."

She kissed his cheek and said a quiet, "Thank you."

He went back downstairs and found Deputy Turner standing by the Tobiano when he came out.

"Thought I'd see you off," Turner said, as the two men shook hands.

"Sounds like your boy's going to be all right," Clint said. "I'm glad."

"So am I," Turner said. "I just gotta make sure he has his head on straight when he gets back on his feet."

"I'm sure you'll be able to do that," Clint said.

There had been a few people on the street when Clint got to the hotel, but suddenly it was empty.

Both Clint and Turner looked up the street, saw five riders coming toward them.

"This don't look good," Turner said.

"Might as well meet this head on," Clint said. "They've got to be here for me."

"The word hasn't gone out yet that the bounty's gone," Turner said.

"I'll see if I can convince them," Clint said. "You might as well go inside."

"I'll stand with you," Turner said, "just in case."

"Thanks."

Clint and Turner walked out into the center of the street and waited for the riders to reach them.

The five men, all wearing dusty trail clothes, and holstered pistols, reined in and stared at the two men.

"What's this about?" one of them asked.

"That's my question. I'm Deputy Turner. What can we do for you gents?"

"This ain't your business, Deputy," the man in front said. "We're here for Clint Adams. We hear there's a big price on his head."

"You heard wrong," Turner said. "That bounty's gone."

The five men looked at each other.

"He's dead?" the front one asked.

"No," Clint said, "I'm right here, but there's no more bounty."

"Is that so?"

"Yes," Clint said, "it's so. You boys should just turn around and head back the way you came."

"That doesn't sound like somethin' we should do," the man said. "I'm thinkin' you're lyin' to try and save your skin."

"Go over to the bank and ask, if you want," Clint said.

"Naw," the man said, "I think we'll just get it done right here and now."

All five men went for their guns, leaving Clint and Turner with no choice. They drew and fired. Going over it in his mind some time later, Clint realized he got three of them, while Turner got the other two. Whatever shots the five men got off went straight into the ground, or into the air, as they all went flying from their saddles.

Clint and Turner both ejected their spent shells and reloaded as they walked among the bodies, checking.

"All dead," Clint said. "Looks like I'm leaving you with another mess."

"It was their call," Turner said, holstering his weapon.

Clint did the same, then looked at Turner.

"Looks like your boy was right."

"About what?"

"He said you were faster than he was," Clint said. "That was impressive."

"I was a little behind you," Liam said, "but that's what happens with age."

"You sure you don't want me to help you clean up?" Clint asked.

"I'll get some men over here to do it," Turner said. "I think you and Windham have had enough of each other."

"I think you're right."

Clint walked to the Tobiano and mounted up. As he rode out, he hoped the word would get out about the bounty being off him, real soon.

Coming July 27, 2021

THE GUNSMITH
472
THE TRACKER

**For more information
visit:** www.SpeakingVolumes.us

On Sale Now!

THE GUNSMITH *series*
Books 430 – 470

**For more information
visit:**

On Sale Now!

THE GUNSMITH GIANT *series*

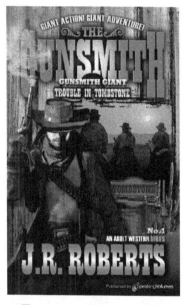

For more information
visit: www.SpeakingVolumes.us

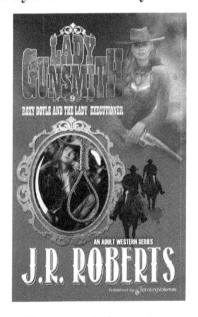

On Sale Now!

TALBOT ROPER NOVELS
by
ROBERT J. RANDISI

For more information
visit: www.SpeakingVolumes.us

On Sale Now!

**Award-Winning Author
Robert J. Randisi (J.R. Roberts)**

**For more information
visit:** www.SpeakingVolumes.us

www.ingramcontent.com/pod-product-compliance
Lightning Source LLC
Chambersburg PA
CBHW030055210525
27031CB00027B/147